EBURY PRESS

YOU ONLY LIVE ONCE

Stuti Changle is a bestselling author. Her other novel, *On the Open Road*, traces the journey of three twenty-somethings who have just quit their jobs to follow their dreams.

Stuti quit her corporate career to inspire people by sharing life-changing stories. She is often invited by prestigious institutions for speaking engagements, where she encourages young people to follow their dreams. She made her TV debut in 2019 as a host of the TV series *Kar Ke Dikhaenge*.

A seeker of endless experiences on her quest to share life-changing stories, she wishes to travel to the extreme corners of the world before she dies. Every year, Stuti spends time in the coastal village of Palolem in Goa. She is currently based in New Delhi, where she lives with her husband, Kushal Nahata, co-founder and CEO of FarEye.

She loves to connect with her readers. Talk to her on

Instagram: @stutichangle
Facebook: stutichangle1
Twitter: Stutichangle

To stay updated on events, book tours, speaking engagements, storytelling workshops, readers' meet and greet, press releases and blog posts, subscribe at www.stutichangle.com.

T0298288

you only live once

One for Passion
Two for Love
Three for Friendship

STUTI CHANGLE

EBURY
PRESS

An imprint of Penguin Random House

EBURY PRESS

USA | Canada | UK | Ireland | Australia
New Zealand | India | South Africa | China

Ebury Press is part of the Penguin Random House group of companies
whose addresses can be found at global.penguinrandomhouse.com

Published by Penguin Random House India Pvt. Ltd
4th Floor, Capital Tower 1, MG Road,
Gurugram 122 002, Haryana, India

Penguin
Random House
India

First published in Ebury Press by Penguin Random House India 2021

16

ISBN 9780143453581

Typeset in Sabon by Manipal Technologies Limited, Manipal
Printed at Thomson Press India Ltd, New Delhi

www.penguin.co.in

To the ones you've loved. And lost.
Not necessarily to death.

'The world is our home. It is delusional to call your apartment home. Even worse to stick to the same place all through your life. If you've found love or happiness somewhere, you've found a home.'

—Ramy, *On the Open Road*

THE LONGEST FLIGHT

Alara

Friday, 1 November 2019
La Epicurean
Mustek Main Street
Prague, Czech Republic

'I carry a piece of you wherever I go.'

How would you define 'long' in your life? Let us begin with the longest night of your life. When was it? Was it when you had your board exam the next day? Or was it the one when you could not get up because you had partied too hard the night before? Or was it when you dreamt about the love of your life all night?

About meeting them, finally.

How do you define long moments? Would it be in hours, or minutes? Would it be days and days? Months, maybe?

Whatever it may be, long would mean something for you too. For me, 'long' has been as long as the day I was born, and might stretch to the day when I take my last breath. Yes, that is how long it's going to be, the longing to meet my mother, touch her, know her, embrace her, and never let her go.

All through my life, I kept asking Dad, 'What happened to her?' A child without a mother always feels incomplete. It's his unwillingness and reluctance to find her that has ruined my life in several ways.

Living with him is like clinging to a damaged arm. At times, I become the worst version of me. The fascination to not let go is huge, but the perks of actually doing it would be amazing. I find it difficult to imagine my life without him only until I am with him. If I let him go once and for all, I should be able to move on.

But as I grow older, I hope that someday I will be able to forgive him.

A few years back, I found a box full of my mother's unreleased songs in the attic. She was a singer and songwriter. Back in the 90s, she played at The Hippie Trail in Goa and tourists from across the world came to watch her perform live. I carry this box with me. Within me, it's a box full of questions gaining weight every passing day as new questions get added to it.

Where did she disappear? Did she not love me ever?

My dad had moved on long back. It has been 22 years since she left us. I can calculate it exactly as I dress up in a red evening gown to attend his 21st wedding anniversary with Irena, my stepmother. I could never gather the courage to ask whether it was planned or by accident that my father decided to tie the knot exactly a year after my mother went missing, on 1 November 1998. He married Irena in Czech Republic. I have been struggling to establish a sense of belongingness with the country since then.

Czech is beautiful, but I long to visit my roots once. I want to live where my mother spent her childhood, know who she was connected to, how would she spend her weekends, the place where she attended school.

She was a singer, that's all I know, with clarity and confidence, and so am I. It's only when I compose my own music that I travel away from reality and feel that she is standing by my side, holding my hand, forever.

My dad never stopped me from following my passion and so I have found an excuse to forgive him for the mistakes I believe he committed in the past. We don't connect that well, dad and I. My stepbrother Alan and Dad are closer, I feel. More so because Alan's mom is still with him, unlike mine.

I would write through the nights I felt the pain. That's how I composed my first song at the age of eight. My music teacher as well as my classmates broke into tears when they heard it. It was deep, dark, and insane for an eight-year-old to write and sing with such intensity, they believed. That's when and how my career as a singer began.

Irena, my stepmother, is a new-age fashion influencer and helped me set up my *YouTube* channel. She isn't really talented, but she married a wealthy guy, and fancy social media accounts are part of the assets you create if you have a lot of money. After all, rich people can afford to buy new clothes for every post they make.

Having said that, she is a nice person at heart. I don't really hold anything against her.

I'm not close to anyone at home. Not really. I'm close to my guitar. It's because it always meets my expectations. People? They often fail to do so. Unfulfilled expectations lead to unfulfilled relationships.

'Hey! Alara,' says my step-aunt Betty as I enter La Epicurean.

'You've grown up to be a beautiful woman,' she continues.

'Thank you,' I respond. I don't talk a lot when it comes to Irena's siblings. They're five women, full of gossip and unnecessary banter. Also, here in Czech, women outnumber men, so they're on a constant lookout for a foreigner to settle down with. Betty is the youngest one and I heard her own siblings discuss her relationship with a guy from New York who is half her age. He is the one who gave her the name Betty too. Living the American Dream has fascinated the world since the 1960s.

'Which song are you performing tonight?' she asks.

'Time,' I say, wondering if she would even understand the depth of the concept. Time it is, the one thing that has never been on my side. Time is what ruined my game early on. Time is what I challenge as I hope to find my mom, or perhaps, an answer.

'You have not published a new song in months. What keeps you busy these days?' she inquires. 'You don't even have a day job,' she adds.

Yes, this is where I draw the line. Relatives can get so unbearable at times. I am facing a writer's block, I write my own songs after all. What would she know of it? She is the kind who would seek Irena's help to write even an email.

'Soon,' I smile wide. Curt. Short. Sweet. She deserves to know that much.

It's been quite some time since I last published a song on *YouTube*. I wish to release my first album. But I have run out of ideas, literally. I know deep within my heart that leaving this place would help me ideate and write songs. Here, I am consumed with much more than writing and performing at cafes. I have to attend customary functions like today. My dad is respected in the community, and that's the thing about rich people. They never get bored of partying and socializing. Me? I told you, right? I struggle with a sense of belonging.

I long to be myself sans all the responsibilities and sensibilities I find myself compelled to fit into. I long to meet you, mom. Let me tell you, your mother would perhaps be the most overlooked person by you, trust me. You might not even appreciate the food that she cooks with all the love. But there are people like me who don't even know what food cooked with love tastes like. I have only heard about it from other people.

I walk up the stage, set my guitar, and start to sing:

I wish to go back in time
and meet you
when you had not met her!

I wish to hold you and say
pack your favourite things
we are hitting the road, baby!

I wish to kiss you and say
you're everything that
I ever wanted in this life!

If I am madness you are peace, baby!
Then I come back home to reality
a broken guitar, an empty room

You walk back home to her,
your love, your dream!

I wish to go back in time
and meet you
when you had not met her!

While I play, I am mostly looking at the love of my life, my guitar. I lift my face and eyes up to realize I performed to a lukewarm response. Claps—some real, some forced. Smiles—some real, some forced. Thereafter, the entire restaurant is filled with chatter and noises. People get busy getting themselves wine and dinner. Here's where I always make room for sneaking out. I never planned to spend the night here.

Irena's relatives are too pretentious to appreciate my songs. They appreciate mainstream music and whatever is trending. Also, I am not very popular in Czech. I compose in English and Hindi, some of my *YouTube* subscribers are from India.

People often ask me, 'Where are you lost?' Lost is how I feel, mostly. Alien in a room full of people, full of conversations. I long for a sense of belonging. I mostly find it within me, in my imagination, with the people I wish were part of my life, and in places far off that I have never been to. Reality is in stark contrast to what I long for and, therefore, I seek solace in being lost!

I drive back home, walk straight to my bathroom, look into the mirror, and question myself, 'Why? Why did she leave me, abandon me?' I believe that God has been unfair to me. So I don't really believe in his existence. All I know is that if I want something, I will have to go get it for myself. That is how it has been.

But guess what? Tonight isn't for crying. I have done enough of it. Tonight is about making a move. It is time to get going for my life's most awaited trip. Oh wait! Did I forget to mention that I'm travelling far away tonight? Well, yes! My bags and plans are in place. When I step out today, I'm flying off, really far off! I have been planning it for months and it is the perfect day to begin the search.

The only person I know who holds some pieces of my life's greatest puzzle resides exactly where my mother was born—Goa. He must be sipping a glass of beer in Ricky's Beach Shack, his own, onlooking the Arabian Sea. I spontaneously check the shack's story on *Instagram*, and my speculation finds evidence. He indeed is doing that. He does not have a personal account though. Sheen, the cafe manager, handles this. He must be exactly the oldie who feels being on social media is a waste of time. How did I figure it out? I have been stalking this account for over two years now. Who's Ricky? Well, he's my mother's childhood friend. Besides him, there is only that box full of unreleased songs that I have.

For the longest time I had wanted my post-graduation at a local Arts college to end so that I could start making some money. My recent rise on *YouTube* and working part-time as a waitress in Mustek got me enough savings. Then, all I had to do was convince my dad with a beautiful lie—India Music Tour across cafes.

'Leave after my anniversary party. Everyone is looking forward to watching you perform, darling,' he had requested.

'Of course, Dad!' I had grinned. After all, leaving on this auspicious day was part of the plan.

I move into the shower. Let me tell you that the shower is my temple, the place where I worship, not God but the person within me. I have not touched this person ever. Maybe it is what they call the soul. I worship it by either talking to it or listening to it. Soul to us is like the essence of a flower, responsible for its fragrance. Its voice shows me the way to light, and sometimes, the depths of the dark.

I am an atheist, a non-conformist, a dreamer. I don't visit temples made of bricks & mortar when I need to worship. I head to the shower. Before embarking on the pilgrimage of a lifetime, I have to worship.

The shower is where I listen to my soul or talk to it. It feels like the perfect place, devoid of all earthly noises, far off from the not-kept humanly promises. The shower is where I reminisce about all things happy—the sound of my guitar, the bliss of the first rainfall, the intoxication of red wine and the warmth of a cup of hot coffee.

Water, at its every touch, lifts me from the drudgery of life and norms of the society. It heals me, not the tangible me but my soul, this force within me.

The shower is where I have made love from the heart and bled dreams from the eyes.

But tonight, I will tell you more about bleeding dreams than making love. Disappointed you must feel, but I don't have an option, I have to tell my story.

Bleeding dreams isn't just crying. It is not even bleeding, exactly. When you've cried so much that your eyes become red like blood, this is when you're bleeding dreams. When you've tried your best to believe that your dream will come true but can't walk any further, or even crawl any further; this is when you're bleeding dreams.

I have been doing that in the shower, my temple, for as long as I can remember.

Tonight, as I stand beneath the flowing shower and lean my head against the wall, I can feel the heavy sighs. These sighs scream that my chest will explode at any moment, oozing out blood like honey from a honeycomb, becoming one with the flowing water draining into the pipeline.

There's haze in the bathroom, dim yellow lights, the sound of water on marble and a symphony of crickets chirping. It's night. I can hear my breath letting out music similar to that from a broken conch shell—dismal, distressing, and sharp. After all, it is in the company of music that you worship God, or the demon, don't you?

I don't always talk to my soul as I am doing tonight. It is mostly about listening. My soul tells me about the goodness in the world, such as the smell of the ocean far away, where I should be spending my next vacation. It tells me that unlike the place I live in, it rains for hours and hours, the way I like it, in some parts of the world. It tells me that I'm insignificant in this vast universe, boundaries to which could never be known, and that I can calm down, breathe, and then take a step forward. It tells me to help the needy, who aren't half as fortunate as I am, and spend time with them.

It tells me to love my dad, despite everything. Most of all, it tells me to listen to my heart.

Don't forget this one, as I never do, it tells me to listen to my heart. I listen to it bravely and do as it tells me to. Yes, I am the one who listens to my heart.

The shower is where I stand as myself—naked, vulnerable, and all on my own.

You must feel that I am incomplete. But that's not true. I feel complete. But how can one be complete in solitude? Beneath this flowing shower, I feel wholly myself. I feel that I no longer have to dress up like my family wants me to, sing like they want me to, or attend customary weekend social parties like they'd like me to.

I am myself sans all the responsibilities and the rituals they find themselves entangled in. I don't want to fit in. I want to be myself.

I walk out of the bathroom and move to the wardrobe to pick up the box kept amidst my clothes. I pick up a pair of binoculars from the drawer, a pair of slippers from another, and my diary from the bedside.

I had finished my packing long back. These are just some add-ons. But I feel unsettled, anxious that I might still have left something. I scan the room in haste but don't find a thing that I would have missed. Have you ever looked at a room as if it were your last time? Register every single detail of it. I have spent five years in this room. I give a final look to the walls done up by me, and I shut the door.

Before leaving the house I also glance upon my incomplete family photo. Have you ever looked at someone's face so closely as to register every detail of it? As if you know that you are looking at it for the last time? I could never get over the resentment that he never made a bigger effort to seek out the truth. I had to remember my Dad's passive eyes and, of course, his mouth that kept at par with his eyes.

I had to remember every bit of his face.

They say, out of sight is out of mind. If you can forget that 10 Euro note in the pocket of your jeans, you can forget anything until you chance upon it again.

Is holding on difficult? Is letting go easy?

I reach the airport just in time. I could not afford to miss this flight. I am flying out of Europe, all on my own, for the first time. As I make my way towards the check-in baggage counter, I exchange smiles with another girl who seems to be of Indian origin. She seems to be my age and is travelling on her own too.

This girl reaches the counter first. Right behind her, a woman whose shoulder tattoo reads 'Be Kind' shouts at her. She gently smiles in return while offering her to move forward. Now standing right in front of me, she says, 'Nice bag'.

'Thank you,' I reply. No person is bad, how you look at them is a reflection of your own self. A friend of mine would always remember others by the cars they owned, while I never even noticed their clothes. I feel that we must always look up to somebody. Everybody is unique and has something unique to offer. It helps you keep yourself grounded.

'Would you mind me asking where you got it from?'

'Oh! Why would I?' I shrug, 'It's a birthday gift! My father brought it from the U.S.'

'Lucky you! Your dad must be amazing, huh. He must love you so much. What a gift! Perhaps I will never get to know what model it is,' she replies.

'Yeah! It would be kind of rude to call him up and say—Hey! Dad. Where exactly did you get my bag from?' A broken laughter erupts out of me.

We laugh in unison like school children do over the most stupid jokes, and even engage in a high five. To be honest, her innocence reminds me of one of my friends from school. My father kept us moving between cities all through my life and I never got to meet her again. I could never find her on *Facebook* either! But this woman felt like that old friend uniting after years.

I bid her a happy journey as I am now the first person in the queue. She moves towards the boarding gates.

'Hello ma'am,' says the beautiful attendant from the ground staff. Her name card reads Melania.

'Hello, Melania,' I say as I hand her my phone with the flight reservation details.

'Window?' she inquires with a smile. 'Yes,' I say. It's going to be a long flight.

'How many check-in bags?' she asks almost mechanically. I believe that after call centre executive jobs, this one is the most demanding. The most awful tragedies might hit you personally, but you've got to smile still.

'Two.' It's three actually, including the box full of questions in my mind.

'You may place it on the baggage belt,' she says with a smile and adds, 'Happy journey.'

'Thank you!'

Much to my surprise, I find the same Indian girl seated on 18 B, right next to my seat 18A. I put my hand baggage in the cabin above our seats and greet her with a smile, 'Hey, we meet again!'

'Yes, we do,' she chimes.

'So, where are you headed?'

'Goa. How about you?'

'Bingo, Goa actually. I will take the Konkan Kanya Express after we land in Mumbai. It's my first time in

India so I figured I will be able to explore more if I take the train.'

'It isn't going to be easy if you take the train in India,' she adds.

'I will manage. By the way, I am Alara.' I move my hand forward in a friendly gesture.

'Avika,' she says as she shakes my hand.

'Are you a singer or a guitarist?' she asks with curiosity, her eyes like a cute puppy's, her mouth drooling with inquisitiveness.

'I'm a singer and songwriter. Yes, I can play the guitar.'

'I knew it! You know how to play the guitar? How cool is that!'

'Oh no! It is not as cool as it seems to you.'

'Why? And you must have fans? Some of them? Lots of them?'

'Even Elisha has fans. A lot of them. No one knows what happened to her. Sadly, she was not even famous when she was alive,' I drop this name in the conversation to check if Avika has roots in Goa too. Everyone now knows Elisha in Goa.

'She could not keep up with her drug addiction, does it imply that all singers share the same fate?'

'She isn't dead. No one ever found her body. She could be living under a different name, you know!'

'That's just being optimistic. Everyone in Goa believes that she married a rich guy, fled off to live the dream life, here in Czech, found her husband cheating on her and probably tripped on drug overdose before she finally succumbed to death,' she mutters.

While she has all the reasons to believe what the local media reported, years after Elisha disappeared, she has no idea that we're discussing my mother. I want to mention again that they never found her body but the onus of changing the topic is totally on me now.

'I'm not into drugs, thankfully!' I laugh as I make an attempt to take her attention away from Elisha.

'You must have fans though?'

'Yeah! You must also subscribe to my *YouTube* channel,' I suggest to her.

She unlocks her smartphone in an instant and opens up the search panel of *YouTube*. She gestures at me to browse for my channel.

AlaraOfficial, I type and hand the phone back to her. She immediately taps on Subscribe. She then puts my latest song 'Time' on 'listen offline' download. 'I'm going to listen to this,' she smiles.

'What do you do by the way?' I ask her.

'I work as a social media manager for a digital agency. I can skyrocket your follower numbers overnight,' she winks.

'I want to get away from the glare of social media.'

'Oh! Really?'

'Yes, I want to take some time off and work on original compositions. I write and sing my own songs, you know! Creativity is faced with a block when the mind is not free. I want to be free.'

'Your trip is more like soul searching, reflecting! Like one of those Hollywood films. All I can say is that you won't find a better place than Goa. The sea and its vistas are so tranquil.'

'Oh yes, they are! I have seen a lot of pictures online.'

'Reality is far beyond the soulless photoshopped pictures. How can people feed their soul by just stalking bloggers on *Instagram*? I believe you've got to walk out, explore, and come back with your own story.'

'I totally second that.'

The air hostesses start with their demonstration process. As I look out of the window, the jet turbines move in a gigantic circular motion. She plugs in her earphones and tells me that she's listening to my song 'Time'.

I lay my back against the seat. Take-offs don't give me a nice feeling. It's like leaving the land and charting into the unknown. But isn't only when you've exhausted your belief in the known that you look for answers out in the unknown. It's faith, it's belief, that keeps you going. Nevertheless.

The longest night of my life is this long flight where I find myself seated. I feel time to the millionth part of a second. It is like boarding a rocket only to be lost in space, not knowing when I would return. Every second, I see flashes of my past life, here and there.

When I break out of my reverie occasionally, I think of all the reasons why this flight should not spiral down. I am a nervous flyer and no matter how hard I try to lower my anxiety, it wouldn't help. But today, I can't die.

As I look at the baggage cabinet, assured that the box is safe in my backpack, I am reminded of all the years I have waited to embark on this journey. Mom, I carry a piece of you wherever I go. The piece isn't round and smooth. It's scratched and broken. It hurts me as it reminds me of the unspoken words, unkept promises, and uncalled-for advances. It's unbearable to carry it any further. Sometimes, I wish to claw it out and let it sink in the deep sea. I would bleed for a while but eventually I would be set free from the pain of carrying it—the piece of you! Not all pain is physical, not all abuse is physical, some of it is emotional, and I desire to heal—heal by the deep sea, heal beneath the warming sun.

TICKET TO FREEDOM

Aarav

Friday, 1 November 2019
HSBC Bank
Bund Garden Road
Pune, India

'In the quest of getting farther from you, with
every passing day, I got a step closer to myself.'

I travel, when in doubt, when nothing works out, when laughter seems hard, and relationships fall apart! Buying a ticket of the Konkan Kanya Express every Friday night means buying a ticket to freedom for me.

I am a final year engineering student at Goa Institute of Management and Technology who bagged a summer internship in Pune at HSBC in their IT team. I should have been back to my college by November, but my boss Akshaye and the company wanted me to stay. It's a paid internship so neither my college nor I had apprehensions about it. My college's only concern was that the final year college placement season is around the corner. But Askhaye asked them not to worry as he will most likely recruit me in his team.

My boss Akshaye often tells me that hard work can take you places in life. He started as an Airtel sim sales executive somewhere in Nashik, which is far from being the corporate hub of India, and has grown to become the Vice President—IT of the APAC region. Amazing, isn't he?

Three months into the internship, he knew there was something up with me. Maybe the stipend was the only reason I chose to stick around.

There's a lot going on in my head right now. It is not just the career that I'm unsure of, I recently broke up with my college senior and live-in partner, Tara. She is the one I fell in love with on the first day of college, she has been the only one so far. I was meek and shy as a school kid. I was not the kind who would simply approach girls. She suggested that we leave the hostel and move-in together, but is now settled in the UK with her husband. Recent? Yeah, it has been only seven months. College relationships usually only last until the last day of college. Mine was one such relationship for sure.

My weekends meant listening to stories from her, watching *Netflix*, and drinking beer together. Now that I live with a couple of broke bachelors looking for jobs in IT, I don't feel like spending my weekends in Pune. Every weekend that I do, I feel like evaporating into nothingness. Maybe that's the reason I travel, far from my city, to the sea and beyond.

Life has become a party of the kind where you feel deserted in the company of others. Not just plain and simple lonely, but precisely one where you feel hollow, every second. I meditate, I run, I run fast. Then order pizzas at last. I scream, scream harder into the shield of my pillow. Tara, someday I will definitely get over the thoughts of meeting you again.

Tara's wedding was a huge shock and brought out the comic in me. I had always wanted to tell jokes on stage but had repressed my passion for the fear of people not approving of it. After she left, I felt I had hardly anything to lose. I always had a flair for making people laugh, but this time I honestly asked myself, 'Can we celebrate pain?'

Building on the art of comedy is kind of iterative. I can always practice harder and become a better version of me. But relationships bloom and wilt like flowers. Seasons arrive and pass by, and a new flower blooms once the older one is consumed by death. With humans, it's different; they have feet and often walk away much before death. In our case, death did not do us apart, like we often worried when we were still together. As time progressed, life did. I am not in the mood to date a new girl. I believe I have lost the patience to deal with new tantrums. Every relationship is an investment of time, also money, all until you've wooed the girl. Neither do I have time nor money to invest in a relationship.

All I want is to figure out the best career for me and work for success. I have a huge education loan to pay off. My parents are definitely not the kind who can bear the expense of the ever-increasing college tuition fees in India. In fact, my mother is so cautious about every paisa we spend that when I'd go to school she'd ask me not to share the dry fruits with others as they were expensive.

As I move into the conference room to make phone calls, Akshaye passes by in the corridor.

His smile tells me he has figured out that I sneak out to Goa every weekend. When you're hiding something from someone, every encounter feels like the doomsday. You know deep within your heart that someday you will be caught for sure.

So well, a recent development is that I am a part-time stand-up comedian at Ricky's Beach Shack in Goa. I am not a popular one, just an amateur, trying things out. Tomorrow is my second performance. Just in case Akshaye knows the truth, chances are that he has worked his butt twice as hard to dig out the truth. We have not had a real adult conversation about this.

Akshaye has deep green eyes, fair complexion, and a height that complements his Aryan personality traits. He is encouraging, kind, and humble. He slides the cabin door and peeps into the room. 'Lunch at 2 p.m.?'

'Where?' I get excited as I wonder if he's taking me out to the fancy newly inaugurated fine dining restaurant Colorin near our office. He has this habit of surprising the team with elaborate gestures.

'Cafeteria,' he says without an expression and walks off silently.

'I guess he is going to take the information out of me,' I whisper under my breath.

The gentleman that he is, he would be more concerned about me joining a drug cartel than not meeting the sales targets, I know. However, I am never absent at work. So he ideally has no way to raise the topic and warn me against the same. His expressions reveal that finding about my stand-up act in Goa is the only thing.

A poster with an Oscar Wilde quote that reads, 'Be yourself; everyone else is already taken' hangs on a wall of the cafeteria, right below which I sit to talk to Akshaye. I have been looking at the poster since day one. It's funny that this quote adorns the wall of a bank's corporate office where hardly anyone is being themselves.

I point to the poster as I start a casual conversation with Akshaye.

'Be yourself. Am I being myself since the day I started taking my own decisions?'

'You were always being yourself. Even if you're doing what others want you to, you're taking the final call.'

'You mean to say that I'm being myself since the day I was born.'

'Yes.'

'Of course not!'

I wanted to bring a significant change to my life, a change that would empower me to live the way I would love to. But I have had a fading interest in everything. Nothing had excited me for more than a certain time period. It had happened to me in the classroom as well. My love for Math was not natural but fuelled by the fact that my dad would have freaked out if he came to know that I didn't perform well. I would not have been able to get a well-paid job if I dare not be a top scorer in Math. I loved Geography like no other subject, but there were no conventional careers in Geography, not to my family's knowledge at least. Biology had grown on me at one point of time, but the very fact that it would take a huge amount of time and effort to become an established doctor had made me restless for nights after writing the board exams. I loved English as a subject, and the primary reason was the beautiful storytelling it involved. I did a couple of comic mime performances on stage back in school, also wrote a few poems as a young kid, and got some articles published in the magazine at the university. The moment I left school, I wasn't being myself suddenly. I was chasing a career in engineering.

'I am trying to be a version of me that my dad wants me to be,' I say.

'You're always being yourself. I would say it again, even if you're doing what others want you to do, you're taking the final call.'

I remember how my dad, a math fanatic, had once asked me as a child, 'What is the best thing you can do with numbers?'

'I can write jokes on them!' I had replied innocuously. Two slaps followed. No more. No less.

Akshaye is definitely correct. But what's more? Why isn't he coming to the point. I keep wandering my gaze to every nook and corner of the cafeteria.

'What's in your bag?' Akshaye quizzes.

'Umm . . . laptop, diary, charger, yeah,' I take a pause.

'Beach shorts?' Akshaye grins.

'No, uh . . . umm . . .' I wonder what to tell him.

'You must be off to Goa, it's Friday tonight.'

'Why?'

'Why are you keeping secrets?'

'What kind of secrets?'

'When people answer questions with a question, they're definitely hiding something.'

'That must be your definition.'

'Getting defensive too.'

'I'm not.'

'You are.'

'Actually, I perform at . . .'

'Ricky's Beach Shack,' he completes my sentence.

'How do you know that? Besides, I am allowed to do anything on the weekends. I am not making any money from it, so by contract the company can't sue me.'

'Oh! I wanted to congratulate you, little boy. I'm happy you're getting over the Tara episode. Besides, I know Ricky runs this place.'

'You've got to answer this right now. How do you know this and that?'

'Ricky called me up this morning.'

Gosh! Ricky can be so unpredictable at times. 'Sir! He is a retired psycho, but he is good at heart. Don't mind anything he says. He's just helping me cope with the breakup.'

'Of course, I wouldn't. I am happy that a stranger isn't keeping secrets, unlike my own *bachcha*,' he laughs. 'Besides, Ricky sounds like a gentleman.'

'Have you finalized tomorrow's script?' he continues.

'No, I will do it in the bus. That's why I take the bus. It helps me write and travel at the same time.'

'Why don't you perform here at office? We will pay,' he winks.

'Someday!'

'You've a meeting with my boss at the head office near CST station in Mumbai at 5 p.m. The cab is waiting downstairs. Get going!'

'Sir, but I have to reach Goa.'

'By Konkan Kanya Express, right?'

'I didn't get you.'

'Here you go.' He hands me a ticket. 'The office will pay for the cab to Mumbai.'

'Akshaye, why did you do this?'

'I'm just making it easier for you.'

'Thank you, sir! You're the best!'

'You're a rock star!' he chimes.

I live with the burden of my dreams, with a burning desire to reach out to millions. I have started to find bliss in this quagmire, for it acts as a fuel to keep me moving. Every day. Every time. If there wasn't a thing to fight for, I would become stagnant, a living dead, like a million others who fit in and don't dare to be themselves. I believe that death should come only when I've exhausted my fuel.

I call up Ricky as I pack my stuff at the desk and move towards the cab. He doesn't even have a smartphone. Calling on the club's landline number is the only option.

'Hello,' Sheen, the club manager, responds from the other end.

'Hello! Can you please call Uncle Ricky?'

Next, I hear Ricky's ever-enthusiastic voice, 'Hello, dude!'

'Uncle, why the heck did you tell my boss about my gig?'

'I want you to be honest to everyone. You need not hide your passion for telling jokes. It's a story that needs to be told out loud.'

'I can help myself. Please don't do this again. You have put my job in jeopardy.'

'That's the idea. I want you to move to the club full-time. I will try my best to keep doing that.'

'I'm fortunate that Akshaye is unlike other IT team leads who suck the blood out of their team members.

He's arranged for a meeting near the station to help me reach Goa.'

'By the way, you've got another surprise waiting for you.'

'What's that?' I inquire.

He hangs up on me. Uncle Ricky has helped me in a lot of ways. I owe him big time for being so supportive of my art. But he tends to act weird at times. What scares me more is his love for alcohol. I want him to die a happy and peaceful death, which he claims that he will, but I somehow don't find myself convinced of that.

Uncle Ricky never got married. At the peak of his youth, he was a drummer at The Hippie Trail Cafe and has performed percussion with the famous Elisha. Elisha is one of the finest singers Goa has ever had, but she disappeared in the late 90s. Unfortunately, people discovered her music days after she passed away.

What happened to her? Everyone has their own theory, but no one has an answer. Ricky's Beach Shack often plays her music. Her songs transform you to fight for your dreams, stand up for who you are. She was definitely ahead of her time and her songs will continue to inspire millions for ages to come. That's the thing about art. It never dies. I want to make people laugh. That's all. I wish I could have met her once. She must have been an amazing personality.

I manage to finish the meeting just in time and reach the railway station. It's almost 10:45 p.m. and the train leaves in another 20 minutes. I start looking for my coach, B3. A distressed girl asks in a slightly broken Hindi, 'Where do I check-in my baggage?'

Her question confirms my speculation that though she looks Indian she must definitely be an NRI. What's more, she is travelling by train for the first time.

'We don't check-in here. You have to carry it with you.'

'Where is coach B6?'

I point in the opposite direction, as we're standing somewhere near B4. 'My name is Aarav,' I say, only to realize that she has already left hurriedly in the pointed direction. Unperturbed, I drag on towards my own coach. I settle my bag on the side upper berth and roll my side of the windows up.

The screen of my smartphone flashes: Dad Dad Dad. Why on earth is he calling?

'Hello.'

'*Beta!* Why did you not take the video call?'

I know for certain by now what Ricky's surprise is! I check my phone to evaluate the time I have before the train leaves. Ten minutes! Shit. I have exactly ten minutes before the train engine whistles so loud as to make it evident that I am travelling.

'*Beta!* Think once again,' my dad says. I hear my mom sobbing as if I am leaving this world forever.

33

'What should I tell my friends when they come home for the kitty party?' She continues to sob in the background. I vividly imagine her in mustard yellow cotton saree that she has been wearing for the last 5 years, drenched in tears.

'About what?' I get inquisitive. 'What is she supposed to tell people at the kitty party?'

'*Beta*, a guy called Ricky called me up from Goa. He tells me that you're going to quit your job and join his club full-time as a comedian. When they ask me what does your son do for a living, what should we tell them?'

'He makes people laugh,' I say almost as a reflex. Suddenly, my feet go numb. I realize that my sweet little secret isn't a secret anymore.

'Like Raj Kapoor in *Mera Naam Joker*?' I imagine my mother's face turning pale with a dismal frown. 'Or like Charlie Chaplin?'

My father says assertively, 'Gone are the days of circus, Archana. He is a performer. He will be speaking in front of a huge crowd.' He feeds his ego and continues, 'A start-up comedian, yes!'

'Stand-up,' I almost correct him as a reflex.

'Is it okay if we tell everyone that you've landed a job with Taj Hotel and Resorts in Goa in their IT team. Everyone knows that you are going to get a placement soon and none of our relatives can afford to book the hotel. We'll never be caught.'

'And what will you do when they upload videos on *YouTube*? They will certainly come across it someday!'

'*Beta*, people hardly watch new videos. Sarika aunty has started a food vlog. Last time I checked, it had 600 views, I kept refreshing for 4 days, it now has 601. Moreover, once the ghost of stand-up comedy stops to haunt you, you can get your respectable job in Pune back.'

'Papa! I am not quitting the internship. I will surely get the final offer. Please don't believe in Ricky's cooked up stories. Comedy is a hobby. It's temporary. Passion can't be profession.'

I hang up and set my phone to flight mode.

The train whistles, indicating that it is time to leave. As the train starts to move, I slowly regain my sanity, one breath at a time. My train compartment is a classic scene, as always.

Sitting across from me is an overenthusiastic man who is dumping his religious and political gyan on all. 'Government job? That's the best and the only thing that you must go for!' He shouts like a politician begging for votes. His finger points to nothing in specific but a rust-clad ceiling fan that should supposedly be on a table.

'That's what I told her. After all, she has to get married, look after the babies. Why would she go for a corporate job? Money makes you ambitious,' says the other fellow sitting with his daughter.

'Chai. Chai. Chai. *Kadak* chai,' a vendor passes by yelling.

'One cutting!' I tell him and hand him a 10-rupee note.

'NaMo used to sell chai,' the girl breaks the silence. 'Had he not been ambitious, he would not have become the prime minister of India,' she adds.

'He is a guy,' her father chuckles. I look at his *chappal*s. They're the ones you get from roadside hawkers in Mumbai for peanuts. It reads the logo of *Facebook*.

'What brand is that?' I interrupt him as I sip my glass of cutting chai.

'*Facebook*,' he says with confidence, still puzzled over what my question has to do with his *chappal*s, and of course him.

'*Facebook*'s COO was a woman who recently quit to pay more attention to her own initiative.'

There's pin-drop silence. While the girl smiles as she approves of me, the rest of them now notice my coloured fringes and unconventional features with a distasteful glance. Indians judge you left, right, and centre. Wearing traditional clothes gives you an upper edge. Knowing the local language gives you a faster promotion. These are just a few things to begin with.

A shady guy with unkempt hair on the top berth looks over the entire scene as if he is going to make a feature film on the same. He is probably travelling without a legit ticket. You can tell these people apart by their faces. See? I judged him. I am an Indian too!

A book hawker selling pirated copies of bestselling books passes by. '*Bhaiya*, which book sells the most?' I ask. He points to a title which reads '*Become a Millionaire Overnight!*' We're a population of 1.3 billion, struggling hard to make it big, and most of us want to become millionaires overnight. Especially me. If I could pay off that education loan, I would be free to do anything!

'Do you want any?'

'Yeah. *Become a Millionaire Overnight*,' I say as I hand him a 100-rupee note.

In the compartment next to mine is a family en route to a wedding. I assume that they will probably play *Antakshari* all the way to Goa. Destination weddings are the new 'in-thing' in India. November is the peak of the wedding season. Their children are all over the place, they would keep going up and down on the berths and keep creating a nuisance.

Where do I get ideas for my script? Well, it's all around me. All I have to do is listen.

I rest my head against the window to see the beautiful countryside pass by. Although it's night, the moon is at its brightest best. A train journey is like no other. If you're on-board with your family, it's about deeply bonding with them as the train whistles across the country; if you're on board alone, it's about deeply bonding with strangers and knowing their story. They say time travel isn't possible yet. Physically, yes. However, the moment I step into a train, it takes me back to my childhood. If you're a '90s kid, you know what I'm talking about. Everything—the soup being served with breadsticks, the *chaiwallah*s roaring amidst the hustle, the cutlets, relishing Parle-G dipped in tea, and reading Champak bought from the railway platform of some on route station—it all takes me back to the time of my life that I cherish the most.

After flying for miles in the economy class of various aircrafts, where I feel like a stranger amidst so many sophisticated passengers who would hardly look at each other, a train journey is where I come back home to.

When my day ends, everything fades away, and there is only one thought left, Tara.

Some relationships have a closure. You meet for one last time and end things with a conversation. In my case, it was so abrupt that I never knew when we met last that it was actually going to be our last.

Have you ever stood at the end of a relationship not knowing what went wrong?

Was it their fault? Was it yours?

The older the pyjamas get, the cosier they become. But sometimes you feel like slipping on a pair of jeans. If you stick to the pyjamas for long, you'd never know what breathing in the fresh air feels like. I have put on my favourite pair of jeans, certainly.

I sip my cup of tea and reach out for my pen and scribble in my diary:

I kept shifting apartments
changing cities
in search of a home.
And then,
I found home.
In her.
She didn't.
Life leaves me
with no choice
but to move on.
I move out
yet again
but this time
in search of myself.

The warmth of this cup of tea reminds me of you. Everything around me reminds me of you. I believe it's hard to move on. The more I try to run away, the more I find myself holding on to you. I decide to not give up. I will keep at it—the quest of moving farther from you and the quest of getting closer to myself.

LONG ISLAND ICED TEA

Ricky

Friday, 1 November 2019
Ricky's Beach Shack
Palolem
Goa, India

'Sorrow is an inseparable part of me,
just like happiness.
To live life fully, I believe I must experience it all.'

Life is like a glass full of the cocktail Long Island Iced Tea. It's a mix of the darkness from coke and the golden from rum. And Goa, it's an accumulation of many such cocktails. Goa isn't quite literally a place. Goa is a vibe, Goa is a state of mind, and Palolem Beach in the southern district of Canacona is my hideaway here. Palolem is adorned by hills on one and the horizon on the other side.

No matter the time I go to sleep, I wake up at 5 a.m. sharp. Running every morning by the beachside has been a routine. A waterproof digital watch, a pair of running shoes, a jersey, that's all I need. Why do people seek solace in routine? It is only a thing or two that can spark excitement on a day-to-day basis. Running is one of those activities for me.

When I run, I run religiously. It gives me immense pleasure, and when I get tired it makes me feel as if I have conquered something. It gives me a feeling of achievement. I run every morning without fail and it is something that I have been doing for a long time. There isn't a hurt a morning run can't fix.

I have to shoot for the TV Series 'Sunrise to Sunset' today. It airs every weekend on *National Geographic* during prime time. They're touring the world and featuring the best beach shacks on the show, and we're fortunate that they have picked Ricky's Beach Shack, my own, in Goa. The best part of living in a beach shack is that you can put on your beachwear anytime and move into the inviting ocean, all on your feet.

A team of six arrives at the counter. Four of them are surely the cameramen. An extremely stylish woman introduces herself as Noor. I assume she will walk the talk. We invite them for a cup of coffee, but they suggest to start the shoot right away as they want to capture the sunrise.

In her brief, she tells me to look at her as I answer her questions. It brings me some relief as I am anyway too shy to talk while looking at the camera. It is, after all, my first TV interview.

'Let's start.' She signals to her team and adjusts two collar mics. One on her collar and the other on mine.

'What is a beach shack?' she asks.

'If you'd *Google*, you would find that a shack is a small, often primitive type of shelter or dwelling. Like huts, shacks are constructed by hand using only locally available materials; however, if you ask me, shacks in Goa constitute a way of life. We construct beach shacks every year in mid-October, before the tourist season kicks in, and dismantle them before monsoon. Once the sea water recedes, we build them up again. If you haven't spent a Christmas and New Year at a shack yet, you must book your next right away.'

She asks her cameraman to take a little break and tells me, 'Ricky, you can't be selling your services on the show. It should not look like you're advertising. Don't ask people to book a holiday. If need be, I will say it at the end of the shoot.'

'Okay,' I say as I get a bit conscious. It's my first time and I fear I have nearly ruined it. I take a deep breath and instruct my brain to follow her command.

We continue to walk as we reach the end of the beach. Her team is occupied with capturing sunrise shots.

'There's a jungle echoing with chirping birds on my right. There's a stream of backwater which separates an island nearby, a suitable place for trekking on your own,' I say and point, wanting them to capture the beauty of it all. The camera team follows my command.

'How does it feel to experience the sunrise every morning?' the interviewer continues as the cameras return to face us.

'Palolem has my heart. The sight of the rising sun in between the hills fills me with all the energy and revitalizes my senses. Tourists often enjoy a boat ride on their own or ask the local fishermen who live by the backwaters to take them to nearby beaches or into the jungle via this serene backwaters. If they wish to get the feel of staying on a marooned island for a few hours, they are taken to the nearby Canacona Island. In winters, one might just get lucky and spot a couple of dolphins in the seawater playing and indulging among themselves! Dolphins from places far off migrate here to escape the extremely cold winters, much like my European and Russian guests.'

'Cut,' says a guy from her team. He indicates that we've crossed the deadline for one question.

We take a turn and start walking towards the other end. I complete at least 10 such laps every day. The sea looks tranquil and calm today. However good the change feels, it's not a good thing for the sea to be so quiet. The sea needs to roar to be fine.

Have you ever heard the phrase *lull before the storm*? What kind of storm could be on its way?

'How would you describe the spirit of Palolem? What brings all the guests together?'

'As you can see, the entire coastline is dotted with multiple shacks. After all the good food we serve and the allure of the sea, music is what brings our guests together. During evenings, the entire beach is lit up with beautiful candles that are tactfully placed on the tables arranged right at the beach next to the Arabian Sea. Every weekend, we have live music performances and stand-up comedy acts.'

'What is the most special thing about Goa?' she continues in a hurry. It seems as if the sunrise and sunset are the two most important timings for them.

'When you land here, you experience freedom and peace as you never would have before. After touring around the world for 20 years, I came to settle three years back in this one place I could call home. I was born and raised in Goa. You would think, why is he trying to be cool? Old fellas always retire to their hometowns. While a lot of people dream of owning a beach shack when they retire, I finally do have one. I named it after myself as I haven't met a better person than me, ever. Okay, I'm not that self-consumed, it is only a joke!' I slip into a broken laughter and continue, 'But, to be honest, it was not always the plan. Exactly 23 years ago, I left Goa believing in my heart that this is one place I would never return to.'

I was young, heartbroken, and lost! The only love of my life, Elisha, had left the country with a rich and successful businessman. She probably married and settled down with him in Europe. I never kept contact, and a year later I heard in the media that she had died.

I could never even tell her how much I love her. Oops! 'Loved' her.

Maybe, 'love' her is correct. I don't know. Maybe I did tell her as much in bits and pieces but she never reciprocated. That's the worst part of life. You can't make someone who doesn't love you, love you!

As I answer my guests, I realize that much has changed in these past years. The sea is almost the same, but the coastline feels different now and then. Back in those days, on weekends, Elisha would sing and I would play the drums at the famous The Hippie Trails Cafe.

There was no other shack then. Only locals and hippies knew about this beach. Tourists would go to the more crowded Baga, Calangute, or Anjuna beaches. THT Cafe shut its doors permanently in the early 2000s. I bought the same land three years back and 'Ricky's Beach Shack' was erected here.

Elisha's innocence was like fresh blooming lilies. Of all the dresses she wore, I remember her lilac frock the best. Elisha was this. That. Elisha is to me exactly what your first love is to you. As it remains with you, I could never move on either.

Soon, five-star hotels started to chase us for weekend performances and Elisha became the voice of Goa. Her live performances attracted even Bollywood celebrities, and finally she too received an offer from a big studio in Bombay to record with them.

The only problem with her was, I believe, that she wasn't at all ambitious. She was always more inclined towards starting a family and living a low-key life. The worst thing she did was to leave the country and settle down with that Czech NRI who would visit our shows every week during his stay in Goa. He's the person I have hated the most all through my life. Quite literally. I believe he might have been the reason behind her death. No matter how hard you try, you can't ever tolerate the other person in the life of the person you love.

The worst thing about unrequited love is that you start to compare and make a list of all the things that you could have to get this person. And then realizing that no matter how hard you try, you just can't make the other person love you the way you do. It fills me with deep regret to have not met her once before she died. I couldn't have afforded to go to the Czech.

My life is an open book. I hardly have anything to hide. I still believe that the entire city of Goa knows about my love for her. Maybe she did too.

It's tough to explain why but some relationships hurt until the end.

I knew I was in love because wherever I was I thought of her. To date, when a singer sings his/her deepest melodies in my shack, I think of her. I think about the fact that I could never tell her how much I loved her. When they sing a song, I feel like every note or every word is dedicated to her.

Back then, I was soft and vulnerable. After serving in the merchant navy for almost 20 years, I have become hard as a rock. I still remember every single brutality that I have been through.

Only three months into the job, I was the only Indian sailing with a whole Vietnamese crew to Africa. We had not eaten fresh food in days, and one stormy night a fish made its way onto the deck. Lost she must have been, much like I was in those days.

'Pick it up and butcher it.' Those are the only words in English that I ever heard my captain utter. The rest of the crew started to cheer, as if I was a matador preparing to face the bull. The only difference was that it was a baby shark and I had no red cloth.

My body started to shake and shiver, much like my values, as they force-handed a knife to me. I stared into the shark's eyes. Stone cold they were. It seemed as if it longed to meet a loved one. I could see my own reflection in those eyes. I thrust the knife in its belly, it was dead in an instant, yet I passed out. Two hours later, I woke up in my compartment. The fish had been prepared and served to everyone by then. That day, I knew I would never be the same again. Something in me had changed. Shifted.

I have made all the wealth I wanted. I just want to live my life now. My mother was my only responsibility until the day, during an occasional stop we made at Cape Town, South Africa, I heard that she had passed away while I was still sailing across the Atlantic. My career ensured that I sent money back home to my mother regularly, but it never filled my soul. Now that she is no more and since I never got married, I just have to take care of myself.

I interrupt their conversation and say, 'The sea is my passion. You could do any activity involving water if you visit my shack. When I'm not surfing on the waves, I'm most certainly high on substances my Russian tourists get for me.'

They laugh in unison before I realize that they must have accidentally got it on tape. 'Can we take this off the record?' I laugh.

'Don't worry!' he winks.

If you were to ask me what I liked the best? Marijuana, I would say. One of my favourite varieties smells like flowery incense sticks. All through my life, I tried to run away from this place, Goa. Now, I try to escape the physical boundaries of my very own body. Complicated? You will know more about me as I reveal my story.

Let me make it clear. I am not an addict, I just find bliss in letting myself loose, occasionally.

We keep walking only to reach my shack. The board at the gate reads a new thought every day. It's a typical black board that is looked after by my manager, Sheen. She puts her creativity and fondness for colours to the best use right on this board.

Today, it reads:

Recipe:
Music
Long Drive. Hair let loose out of the window

A bunch of crazy friends
Dish:
A perfect life

Noor alerts her team to take a close shot of the board. She continues, 'What's special about Ricky's Beach Shack?'

'My dream project, Ricky's Beach Shack bustles with people, sounds, and festivity. The only rule is to switch off your phones when you're at the club. I stayed away from a normal habitat and mobile phone networks for so many years that it now suffocates me to the last bit. I find pleasure in little things. Like I find peace in helping newbies learn diving and surfing. I also help young people achieve their goals. When you scuba dive into the ocean you generally have an instructor who guides you all the way to the bottom, hand-holds you, not because you are not capable of reaching the bottom, but to make you realize, when you lose track midway, that you can still achieve it. I am one of those people you meet. Most lost millennials who visit my cafe are living in the FOMO. Somebody got the dream job, somebody got married, somebody is travelling the world, or somebody won an award. It has always been happening. It's just that social media brings it to your notice and you worry for no reason at all. FOMO is useless, unnecessary, and counterproductive. I tell them to stop comparing, start living! But they are more risk-taking and relentlessly pursue their passion, unlike my generation. I envy them for the fact that I was never free. I feared a lot of things in life and, therefore, I was always the follower. People from across the world come to watch my muses perform and get inspired to find their true selves, live meaningful lives, and strive hard to become the best version of themselves.'

'What do sunsets feel like at Ricky's?'

'My tourists savour a glass of wine with delicious food served in the shack, as we offer a multi-cuisine menu to choose from, while listening to their favourite Beatles or Pink Floyd numbers playing in the background. Every Saturday brings a live performance. Evenings are meant to get transfixed by the ambience and feel blessed while you witness a mesmerizing sunset.'

She looks into the camera and says, 'This is just a glimpse of a day that can be spent at Ricky's, but exploring more to land upon new avenues of a perfect holiday is the key to getting more out of this untouched beach village. If you are a social person, like me, you can find travellers and backpackers here from around the world who are willing to share their tales of travel over a mug of beer.'

'You've mentioned that music brings your guests together. What's special about the music here?' she continues.

'Music culture across India means Bollywood. But here in Goa, although only a few miles from Mumbai, we celebrate music spanning across countries and eras. Nothing touches me anymore except for music and some comedy.'

Music reminds me of Elisha, and comedy encourages me to look beyond the tragedy of my life.

I continue after a pause, '*Summer of 69* played on a radio transistor in the background when I met the love of my life for the first time at the school canteen. When you listen to this song, I'm sure you have distinct memories that surface too. Isn't it amazing how listening to the same piece of music takes each listener to a different time zone in their life according to how differently it touched them? Music is that fine invisible thread that connects us to the divine. Music is ethereal. Music is God.'

I still regret not taking up drumming as seriously as I should have. And Elisha, she left an amazing career for nothing! Unlike me, she never returned. I never played the drums after I heard that she died. My drums are still lying at my grandmother's old house in Bambolim.

Elisha chose never to come back, never to keep contact, never to write letters. While she means the most to my existence, I would never want to meet her again, even if she is by any chance still alive. I honestly don't have the courage. I would tremble like a teenager.

All I want to tell you is that I wish I had never met you, Elisha!

I look at the blue sky turning orange as the sun makes its way amidst the clouds. I like the blue sky more. I'm also convinced that my soul is blue. It mingles seamlessly with the blues of the sky, the sea, and the river. My heart feels at home when it feels blue. Sorrow is an inseparable part of me, just like happiness. Life is a mix of happiness and sorrow. To live life fully, I believe I must experience it all.

Sheen smiles at us as we enter the shack and occupy a table closest to the sea. Sheen tolerates all the bullshit I throw at her. Yes, I think she is in love with me. However, I could never feel for her the way I felt for Elisha. And somehow, it doesn't bother her either. She visited my cafe two years back and decided to stay here. She now manages everything as I am hardly in my senses to take control of all this.

'Is one-sided love a bond?' Sheen chimes as she punches our fourth order of the day, my black coffee. I don't have to mention it to her. It's a routine. She gets two cups of coffee for us. Three other tables are occupied already. She often pulls my leg publicly. We often have such conversations. We're like buddies.

'Of course, it is,' I reply out loud as she is still at the counter, about 30 steps away from us.

'Does the hurt get better with time?' she shouts back in a teasing way.

'It helps, as intimacy in a relationship impacts individuality. You don't have to be in a relationship to love someone,' I shout back.

Noor and her team look at us in amazement. I'm sure the kind of things we discuss and talk about, most other people would find shocking.

'Can hurt equal gratification?' Sheen quizzes.

'In this case, it can. What are you high on early in the day? Beer?'

'You,' she winks and laughs out loud. Noor interrupts, 'Is she your wife?'

'We're buddies,' I reply.

'There's so much pain in life. Why not celebrate it instead of crying over it? That's what I tell my boy as well,' I shout out loud to Sheen.

'When is he performing next?'

'Our boy?'

'Yes.'

'Tomorrow!'

'We've sold half the tickets,' she says as she raises her cup of coffee.

'That's good news,' I say.

'We're talking about the stand-up comedian who is performing at our shack tomorrow,' I tell Noor. You must attend the show.

'I am afraid we have to leave back for Mumbai tonight. Perhaps some other time.'

Harinder, our most enterprising waiter, serves us the English breakfast. We talk about Goa for another half an hour as we eat. Noor and her team leave for a day tour and promise to return at sunset for another shoot.

HOMECOMING

Alara

Friday, 1 November 2019
Konkan Kanya Express
Mumbai, India

'There is a reason why we don't have an answer
to everything yet. If we become all-knowing,
the purpose of life will be destroyed.'

People stand up as soon as we land and create a nuisance for the air hostesses. 'Sir, ma'am, please be seated until the captain indicates,' one of them almost screams. After ten minutes, the entire pack is herded on its own. I haven't experienced such a huge mass of people this close! While it's nearly sinful to touch a stranger in Prague, people seem okay about touching each other here as they move out of the aircraft in a haste.

I move towards the baggage belt and wait for my checked-in luggage. The bags are either damaged by mishandling or plastered with poly plastic to protect them. I am the kind who would cover her bag for the fear of receiving them scratched. I get an inexplicable sense of satisfaction in protecting it as if it were my child.

I continue to read 'Lying by the beach in Palolem, Goa' on my favourite blogger Ramy's blog—*on the open road*. It's one of the blogs from India that I religiously follow. Smartphones make sure that you never get bored. Ramy calls them our *Buddy*.

When we were young, Alan and I, dad would take us on road trips across Europe. The one I remember most vividly is where we were traversing the Amalfi Coast with mountains on one and a silver beach line on the other side. We had sent beautiful postcards of those vistas back to our hometown. While Alan sent it to his school friends, I had sent it back to myself. I have a thing for keeping things to myself. I don't really like to share a lot. I believe that if I will not hold on to something for long enough, or strong enough, it will be taken away from me.

Gone are the days of sending postcards. *Instagram* keeps the world updated. But I am going to disappoint my fans. Ramy says that when you are listening to your own inner voice, you have to keep yourself at a safe distance from the outer world. As a YouTuber and musician, my work is open to feedback. Though it is mostly encouraging, I am also faced with nasty posts that ask me to quit singing. When in Goa, I wish to write my own songs and keep away from the virtual world. Ironically, Ramy also suggests that! Days pass and we eagerly wait, but Ramy doesn't post from a vacation.

I write, Off from social media this winter to focus on my creative work, and caption it, Till we meet again! I hit the post arrow.

I switch off the phone and carefully place it in the front pocket of my backpack. There are many smartphones in this world but there is only one you. So, you're precious. Rising to fame in the times of social media can make one delusional at times. Even an ordinary person can be driven crazy by the powerful device, i.e. a smartphone.

Chhatrapati Shivaji Mumbai Airport is a complete mess. When in Czech, I would hardly come across so many people, even on the busiest of days. But Mumbai is madness. People are constantly running, chasing what? One would have to ask a local.

A policewoman swiftly walks towards me. She has the built of a middle-aged guy and a typical Indian face. Big eyes, red *bindi*, and a round face. She gestures at me to move towards a small cabin like room. I follow her.

'What is your purpose of visit?' she asks.

'Umm . . . I am an artist, a singer. I'm travelling to Goa for writing new songs. I needed a break from my routine.'

'Bollywood?' she laughs out loud. 'Another struggler,' she shouts to her colleague and continues, 'When do you plan to leave?'

'Umm . . . I have not booked my return tickets yet. I plan to stay here until the new year. They say the new year is the best time to be in Goa.' I smile.

'Ma'am, do you have a business card?' she asks curtly.

'No! But let me show you my social media account. I have a lot of fans in India too.' I take my phone out and turn it on.

'I don't know about *Instagram* and all!' she says, making weird faces. 'Which songs have you sung?'

'Time,' I say.

She interrupts, 'I will google you! I only listen to Bollywood songs.'

'Oh! Yes, sure. You'll find me. I have sung a rendition of a Bollywood song as well.'

'You may go now.' As I pick my luggage up to move, she interrupts, 'How are you travelling to Goa?'

'By train.'

'Goa Express? Konkan Kanya?'

'Konkan Kanya.'

'You can book a prepaid taxi from the airport. It is safer for foreign tourists.'

'Yes! Sure.' While she is curt and to the point, I feel Mumbai is unlike other metropolitan cities of the world. People do care about others here, even foreigners.

India, I have finally arrived. After months of persuasion and denial, I have finally convinced myself to leave everything behind. Some people make travelling alone sound easy by writing blogs like 'How To Travel The World On Your Own,' but let me warn you, the decision is not that easy.

Extreme winter is about to hit Prague in a short while. It is my favourite time of the year. I know I would not be fortunate enough to witness it. But somehow it doesn't matter anymore, nor does my life back there, which had become a song of monotony. It had nothing more to offer. But it is not my Dad's fault. Maybe, it is my mistake that I could never feel a sense of belonging there.

I wanted to break free as soon as I could but was not able to do it for a very long time. As I pick my baggage and fasten the backpack across my waist, I truly feel that I have successfully left it all behind and that I am moving ahead. The four lines that inspire me a lot keep flashing in my mind. It is the power of weaving words like magic that I have to heal, live, sing, and empower.

I head towards the railway station. On reaching there, I take a sweeping glance of the station to have a panoramic view, only to figure out that Konkan Kanya Express, my saviour, is ready for departure. I am free by all means.

Upon entering the train, I manage to take three selfies! One of the challenges that you face on a solo trip is getting a perfect picture of yourself. Sticks and stands do help, but I'm far too lazy to add those to my backpack. I like to keep it simple and minimal with only the bare essentials to spend my days.

The train whistles goodbye to the platform. We travel to make the most of our lives. We travel to break free from the shackles of society. We travel to explore the bigger plan that we are a part of. Sometimes, we travel to explore the infinity within us.

Stuti Changle

People always ask me, where do I find my inspiration? Travel, I can vouch for it with all my heart. This Friday night is a rare bliss, and I am going to make sure that I spend most of it writing songs. What do you plan to do when you travel? To aid my creative process further, it starts to rain. Rainfall ignites a flame in every soul. A singer is no exception. Children jump with joy, thrill, and go berserk in the rains. Rains lift us with joy, with energy.

I scribble in my diary:

Heaven is white
only in fiction.
It is certainly blue
and green in reality.

What's your drug?
Mine is the sea, rains.
What's your drug?
Or the mountains.

Heaven is white only in fiction. It's certainly blue and green in reality. And when you feel so, you don't really have to die to reach heaven. You can do so while you're still alive. Life is uncertain. But death is certain and no matter what you do, it will meet you someday, somewhere. What happens after death is a complete mystery. So live life to the fullest and visit heaven more often.

Next morning, the first thing I try out is a 'cutting chai', as they call it in India. A group of singers enter the compartment. They're all dressed up in intricate cotton lehengas and dhotis. Women are adorned in black metal jewellery and have designs made out of *bindi*-like dots across their face. They also have on white bangles broad enough to fully cover their wrists and partially even their arms.

They play instruments that are perhaps indigenous to the Indian subcontinent. They sing in their melodious voices. I'm a Bollywood fan so I have never had issues understanding Hindi. Dad made sure I also learnt speaking Hindi, my mother tongue. There's an inexplicable feeling about getting under the skin of a culture.

As I listen to them play *Udd Jaa Kaale Kaawa*, I feel the grief of separation flow in my veins. They are some traditional folk performers and I barely know them. But aren't we all the same? Yes, we are! The core of us is all emotions, feelings, and experiences. How we look or where we come from might differ, yet we're all the same. Humans are all the same. We're like light, omnipresent and ever moving. Love is the infinite space where we are travelling like beams of light.

I ask the little boy in the group of six, 'Where are you from?'

'Jaisalmer,' he says.

They had travelled all the way from Jaisalmer to perform in trains. I'm not sure if they are allowed to. Is it a crime, to express your heart and earn a living? Maybe not. It is way better than begging.

In Prague, many artists travel from Ukraine to sing at tourist locations and earn a living. They sing their hearts out, make people dance, and earn a living by it.

Different countries. Different artists. Different times of the day. Different religions, races, and what not. Yet, they're one, going through the same, feeling the same, bathing in the same river of emotions.

Aren't we all the same? We've all loved. We've all been hurt. We've all longed for our dreams. We've all succeeded. We've all failed. We've all laughed and we've all cried.

As I get down on the platform at Madgaon Junction, I smell and taste the salt in the air. That's the thing about the sea. You can't ignore its presence.

I pre-booked an *Oyo* room near Palolem Beach for two days, it's a budget accommodation. Thereafter, I need to figure out a more economical option, like a backpacker's hostel or a PG.

There is no plan, no place that I know as much as I know Ricky's. It feels kind of weird taking the local taxi. A previous trip to London grants some familiarity with the left driving, but the animals on the road are a complete shock. My driver moves zig-zagging through the obstacles and I let out a gasp for the fear of him running over the cows and dogs and what not! Who likes to drive straight? We love to drive like snakes, and therefore risk has allured mankind for too long.

When the lady on *Google Maps* announces, 'You've arrived,' I almost feel as if life has given me a second chance!

I check-in to my room. It's only big enough for a person to fit into. Today is going to be different than any other day in my life. I look into the mirror to reassure myself that no matter what happens I will be the sole decision-maker of my life and do what I want.

After getting bored for about an hour, I finally find a way out. Actually, not me, but the digital slave in me. *Google* is going to be my saviour today. I turn my smartphone on and search for the dumbest thing someone could attempt.

How to spend time alone?

It is funny how *Google* gets back to me with search suggestions I never thought could exist. It ranges from How to kiss? to How to lose weight? I read a couple of blogs on How to spend time alone? to reach a conclusion. Most of them suggested reading a book.

I move out and enter Cafe Helsinki, which is hardly five minutes of walking from my hotel. I revel in the smell of coffee. There's a bookshelf at the other end of the cafe. I haven't read a good book in quite some time and didn't even bring any with me! How pathetic.

I am educated but have never found good company in books.

A biography gets boring, a travel memoir seems fun, a love story upsets. I decided to read some inspirational stuff. Yes. It should be in the contemporary setting. I have no name. A book catches my attention, enlisting the adventures of an Indian explorer—Ramy. It sounds familiar. I pick the book without giving it a second thought.

This is going to be my very first solo date. I have always been to cafés with either clients, friends, or my boyfriend. For the very first time, it is me, just me.

After reading a couple of pages, I already feel a bit better. I do make sure that I carry my diary everywhere I go as it offers me the luxury of writing songs each day, and probably record my dream album someday.

I stay at the cafe until 4:30 p.m. Later, I march out onto the street, only to discover Palolem Beach. The reception manager had insisted that I don't miss the sunset there, and more importantly I have to find Ricky's Beach Shack.

As I walk by the beach, I find the sea calm and serene. I befriend two Israeli tourists and one of them turns out to be a photographer. I click their pictures and they return the favour. Since my phone is off, they promise to email them to me. They note down my email address.

As I walk further, I come across Siddhivinayak Art shop. A local craftsman is seated there along with his mother, probably the artist of the beautiful paintings on stone and postcards on display. I make sure that I buy from the locals to encourage their art and play a small yet significant part in contributing to their livelihood.

I keep moving along the beach towards the less crowded corner. A couple—probably Malaysian tourists, their t-shirts read so—ask me to click their picture. We instantly strike a bond, engage in casual chit-chat and get a picture clicked together. They also promise me to email them later.

I open my diary and scribble. *Still looking for Ricky's Shack in the intervals. Where are you, Ricky?*

A young girl, probably in her teens, approaches me. She smiles from a distance, too hesitant to come near me. I smile back and continue to write in my diary. As I look up, she is still standing there.

'Hey! What's your name?'

'Parvathi,' she chimes.

'Why don't you come here? Sit with me?'

'Can I?' she asks. Her innocent eyes look kind and full of aspirations.

'Hey! So my name is . . .' I move my hand forward as she interrupts, 'Alara.'

'How do you know?'

'I follow your music on *YouTube*.'

'Really?'

'I am your fan. Your music reminds me of Elisha.'

'Who is she?'

'You don't know her? She's one of our best singers. Goans still love her. You must listen to her songs.'

'Where do I download them?'

'Oh no! She was more like a live performer of original compositions. She never recorded for a music studio. Some recordings are available on the internet, but they're not very clear. There's a place called Ricky's Shack at the end of the beach. Ricky has some good recordings as he was the drummer of that band. However, he is a psycho and you're supposed to switch off your phone before entering. So the only way is to spend an evening there,' she points to the end of the beachline as she talks.

'Can you do me a favour?' I ask her.

'Yes, only if you share an autograph of you,' she says cheekily.

'Of course!'

'Tell me?'

'Don't tell anyone about my arrival here.'

'What do you mean?'

'Don't tell anyone that I am famous on *YouTube* and all of that. I want no public attention. Is that okay?'

'It's a deal.'

She doesn't know that my autograph is a bait to trick her into helping me explore the beach, and also reach Ricky's!

'It's Saturday night. Let's go to Ricky's. I'm sure you will like the place.'

'Okay,' I say hesitantly to her, but bubbling with happiness within.

Oh mother! I wish they play your songs tonight. There is a reason why we don't have an answer to everything yet. If we become all-knowing, the purpose of life will be destroyed.

NEW INNINGS

Aarav

Saturday, 2 November 2019
Ricky's Beach Shack
Palolem
Goa, India

'Often, falling in and out of love happens
simultaneously, with different people though.'

Goa is drop-dead gorgeous. Goa is a reflection of your mood. If you're happy, it feels like a happy place, if you're sad, it feels dark and gloomy. Every encounter in Goa feels new, different. For me, living by the beach is the same as living life like a slow-burning candle. Today feels like one of those days when you prefer listening to the radio for the element of surprise rather than playing your long-lost playlist.

My *Tinder* shows 10 odd profiles and, like every other day, I swipe all of them left. My smartphone rings. 'Happy Birthday!' says the lady at the other end.

'Thank you!'

'You can avail 800 credits on *MakeMyTrip* for your next booking.'

So, here's the deal. It is not my birthday today. I am signed up with more than 15 online travel companies and I have mentioned a different birthdate on each one of them to avail the birthday month benefits every month and ride for half the price to Goa. Young and broke college students often do that.

Switch your phones off before you enter, reads a big board in front of Ricky's. I clearly remember noticing this when I had accidentally landed at Ricky's for the first time.

'Look who is here,' uncle Ricky hugs me and pulls me out of my reverie. Sheen smiles from a distance. She's busy attending to some European clients.

'Hello, uncle! Why did you tell everyone about my stand-up gig? Why can't you keep your mouth shut?' I say as I place all my stuff in the coco hut. Uncle Ricky makes sure to reserve it for me before I reach.

'Fear. No Fear. No Fear. Say this out loud,' he laughs.

'Wow! Is this Elisha's song playing?'

'Yes!'

'Why don't you share this playlist with me? It is not on *YouTube*. I love her voice.'

'It's my prized possession. Nobody can have it.'

Elisha became my favourite singer the moment I listened to her first song. I can listen to her songs on and on. They give me the power to live, to believe in my dreams, and to dare to fall in love again! I wish I could meet you at least once, Elisha!

'All set for the performance?'

'A little nervous, as we've sold tickets this time.'

'That's a good sign!'

I head towards the stage. It's still an hour before I start performing, but I like familiarizing myself with the performance space to deal with stage fright. While I am still practising in front of a few people seated at Ricky's, a girl smiles at me from a distance. She's here with a friend probably. Ricky and the girls are having an animated conversation. Her smile feels familiar and comforting. Oh! I recognize her from the railway station. I feel compelled to go and speak to her.

As I reach closer to her I notice that she's wearing a black dress, smells amazing, has red lipstick on, and just a lean choker around her neck. It is dull golden colour and perfectly complements her skin that resembles ripe blossoms of wheat shrubs. She picks up a glass of water placed on the adjacent table, takes a sip, and places it back. Try this, look into someone's eyes when they drink water, they look inexplicably innocent. When I look into someone's eyes, I know exactly the kind of people they are. She isn't the kind who would hide her insecurities behind her heels.

'Hello,' I say as I break into their conversation.

'Have we met before?' the girl chimes.

'Yes, at the railway station.'

'Oh, yes! Thanks for helping me out.'

'By the way, my name is Aarav. I am performing tonight. I am a . . .'

'Novice stand-up comedian,' Uncle Ricky interrupts and continues, 'Why don't you perform tonight? If we like it, you can perform every Saturday.'

For Ricky, flirting is not sacred. It is not only her with whom he would flirt. He would do this with every woman who crossed his path. Being straight, he could only cajole the guys, like me. This inclination of his was more towards tourists though. His can be termed a personality with congenital flirting disorder. He could have started flirting as early as he was a zygote. He must have winked at the gynaecologist every time his mother went to a clinic for an ultrasound. Although he is jaunty and carefree at heart, I do not like him for his flirting obsession. He flatters everyone and can keep people happy with this idiosyncrasy of his. He is smart, intelligent, and ambitious. He smokes all day long, I suppose, except for when he sleeps. The only thing I admire about him is that he is supportive and encouraging of me.

The girl turns to look at me now. 'Alara. My name is Alara,' she says and continues, 'Sure, Ricky! All thanks to Parvathi for guiding me to this beautiful place.'

Parvathi interrupts, 'My pleasure! Your voice is magical.' Saturday night is a busy affair at Ricky's. By the time we start, the entire shack is bustling with chatter.

Alara is our opening performance for the night and I feel the most excited to watch her perform. She walks up the stage, adjusts her mic, clears her throat, and starts to sing:

In my dream,
you are real.
More than my body
I touch yours,
more than my existence
I feel yours.

In reality,
you are a dream.
Far-fetched, deceitful
alluring still.

Fortunately,
the dream is everlasting
And the reality
Ever-changing.

Music is one of the best ways to heal. When I am not travelling, music transports me to places and makes sure that I am still moving. As I watch her perform, Alara is all that I can think of. I'm sure others feel the same too.

She is like the madness of a club. She does not fit into the conventional definition of beautiful. Her eyes aren't blue, just plain black, nor are her hair coloured differently. Her skin is the colour of sand; not jasmines, lilies, or roses. Her body doesn't resemble an hourglass. Yet, she is so beautiful. Her voice is as smooth as butter and as sweet as honey. I have always been the listen-to-music kind, but tonight I have become the listen-to-words kind.

Appreciating someone's outer beauty without diving deep into their soul is like appreciating honey for its golden colour and not its sweetness. For me, it is sweetness over colour, always!

While I thought I would never be able to fall in love again, she gives me a reason to believe otherwise. Life is strange. Often, falling in and out of love happens simultaneously, with different people though.

She walks down the stage and wishes me luck. I find myself still full of fright and not even half as confident as she had been out there.

As I get onto the stage, the lights on the audience become dim and the focus is on me. While others can now have a perfect look at me, I can perfectly see every nook of Ricky's. I freeze. I want to speak but can't remember a single joke I had prepared. Suddenly, I forget everything and go blank.

I think of my first time at Ricky's. It was raining heavily. I had stepped out of my cab only to see that the lane was flooded, so much so that even the puddles could not be spotted. I felt that I had to be wary of each step I took in this unpredictable circumstance, much like life itself.

The most prominent thing that my eyes instantly took to notice was a board adorned with small neon lamps all around it that read 'Ricky's Beach Shack.' As I had no idea of what to do next, I started taking long strides towards that alluring shack without another thought.

The rain had not stopped yet. It could precisely be termed as a sudden downpour, especially the kind that forces people to stay indoors. Water was gushing beneath my feet. The pure white shirt that I had put on some four hours ago right before leaving my hostel had turned translucent.

My choice of ensemble reflected my sanity, and it was mid-March, a month usually expected to bring with it scorching sunlight. The bizarre change of weather would definitely have made one question my sanity, as my clothes were now dirty as mud and I could claim without a mirror that I looked awful.

While walking towards the shack I heard lightning and thunder so close to my heart that, for a fraction of a second, I thought that my smartphone had exploded inside my pocket. The thought did not seem strange to me anymore as in the past week my smartphone had beeped a million times with tons of messages—devastating ones, no calls though.

People huddled under the shade of shops or restaurants, having been caught unawares by the rains.

All shelters seemed crowded, with no place for solitude, something I aspired to find at the shack. With tapering hope, I pushed against the door and stumbled into Ricky's.

Much to my surprise, the shack played 70s classic rock hits, a phenomena you are least likely to come across these days as there is mostly pop or EDM playing at shacks. I would have loved the ambience otherwise as I am fond of beer as well as the song that played in the background, 'Eye Of The Tiger,' but it was different today. I could not rejoice in the rains as much as I otherwise do, as my thoughts were preoccupied with Tara whom I was dying to see, meet, touch, and what not.

She hadn't called in days. She had just sent WhatsApp messages that felt unfamiliar.

She had not let me sleep for almost a month now and my anxiety rose exponentially with the days that passed by. Needless to mention, I felt tired and exhausted, so I decided to get a coffee. I paced towards the counter to get it. The guy at the bar looked as if he was in his early 20s, probably an undergraduate student from a putative college like mine, working here part-time only to fulfil his desire of being independent in a developing country like India.

I appreciated his courage for having taken on a lesser-appreciated role, though unfairly so, for the sake of this desire.

While I stood in queue, waiting for my turn, I glanced around the shack. The shack was predominantly occupied with couples and tourists. Only a few people in groups of three or more were present. It was crowded and confirmed my speculation and it was hard to find a secluded place here.

To my surprise, I did locate a table in a corner that was fairly away from the dense crowd, but still couldn't save me from all the noisy chatter.

I desired for such a place, not so much to keep away from the noise, but to find an escape from the people so they didn't catch me bursting into tears, which I knew could happen at any moment and I didn't want to hold people's unwanted attention.

While I was lost in my own world as usual, a middle-aged man of athletic built approached me. His calves seemed as strong as the rocks by the beach. He said, 'Did you recently break up?'

Everything about him was moderate, except for the simple audacity of raising such a question, or even to know something of this sort at first glance.

'Who are you?'

'I'm the owner of this place.'

'Ricky?' Having stayed in Goa for three years by then, I was familiar with Goans naming their establishments after themselves.

'When did this happen?'

'What?'

'The break up?'

'We have not broken up. Why would you care?'

'It looks like you aren't sleeping well. Coffee is more expensive than beer in Goa. If you're ordering that, something is definitely up with you! Better for my business though,' he chuckled and left.

'Creepy fellow!' I sighed.

As I sipped my cup of coffee, the song in the background changed to the cult classic '*Let It Be*' by The Beatles. I took out my smartphone from my pocket. It was something I had longed to do in the past few minutes as I was keenly waiting for Tara's call; she had promised that she would call.

I hadn't taken a look at the notifications in the last ten minutes due to the hasty march towards the shack, as opposed to the past few weeks when my average rate of checking the cell phone was an incredulous 100 times a minute, except for the three hours of sleep at night, enough for a person to be termed as deranged. I was not deranged—just an insomniac, or so I told myself to not end up questioning my rationality every few seconds.

One New Message, the screen read.

I tapped the app icon with the excitement of a small child poking soap bubbles blown by roadside toy-vendors at tourist places such as The Gateway of India. However, it was not Mumbai and I was not a child, but all I was here with was immense hope.

It's not working anymore. I am getting married.
All the best.

Tara's message had hit me right here, at this place. It felt like the world had collapsed around me. I couldn't feel my feet.

The more I got to know her, the less I wanted to know. I had known exactly what her desires were, who she had once wanted to become, and who she was trying to become now. Then, I heard from her that afternoon, not any other, that summer afternoon.

After two years of ordering her favourite dish, I ordered mine. A few minutes later, Ricky returned. This time, I couldn't stop myself. I got up and hugged him, my face pressed against his huge athletic body. In that moment, the fact that Tara had left me overpowered my fear of people seeing me cry. I clung to Ricky like yeast clings to bread, it did not feel unnatural.

I said, 'I don't desire anything now. I am a loser.'

Uncle Ricky told me, 'I had always wanted to build a space that looks just like this, one that gives people the creative freedom to think, away from the madness of the new metropolitan areas, for people to be able to break free from their constrained lives and pursue new ideas, ideas that could have an impact, ideas that could change the world.'

'I feel I have lost it all.'

'Everyone you feel is successful now made a start someday. That someday could be today for you.

Whether you want to start a business, get an admission in your dream college, sing a song, or make a million dollars; you will have to start somewhere. Go for it! Now. That's all,' he reaffirmed.

When I didn't stop sobbing, he interrupted, 'Why are you hiding your face?'

'People are going to think that I have gone crazy.'

'When you laugh a lot, they call you crazy. When you cry a lot, they call you depressed. When you speak a lot, they say you should maybe speak less, and the list goes on and on. No matter what you do, they'll put a label on you. But when you know who you are, it really doesn't matter what label they put on you. I'm wild and crazy, yes! But I'm free. That's how I love to label me!' he giggled.

'You're correct, stranger . . . uh oh, Ricky,' I whispered under my breath.

'What are you passionate about? What gives you real contentment?'

'Making people laugh, cracking jokes.'

'Are you sure? You're the one who is crying.'

'Oh! Yes. I used to be a jolly guy. I am a loser now.'

'Choose carefully what you believe in. Your beliefs can either limit you or set you free. You're only as good as you think you are! You have the capacity to make people laugh and cry as an artist. Visit me when you feel better. I might have something for you!'

'Hmm.'

'Remember, when you know who you are, it really does not matter what they label you.'

Releasing my pain through tears was like reaching an orgasm. Only better. When I washed my face I felt stronger. It felt like all the negativity had been washed off. When I walked out of Ricky's and decided to breathe in the fresh air again, it felt glorious.

Soon, Ricky's became that one place I would go back to every weekend, whether I was happy or sad. I didn't realize when the stranger Ricky became Uncle Ricky. He made sure that I performed my jokes in front of others. Tonight is my second performance. He wants to hone me into a star stand-up comedian. But I don't know if I will ever be able to live up to his expectations!

THE NEW GIRL

Ricky

Saturday, 2 November 2019
Ricky's Beach Shack
Palolem
Goa, India

'Vulnerability is your strength.'

'This new girl Alara is performing really well,' Sheen says as she walks up to me. 'She is good for our weekend business. You must ask her to perform every Saturday,' she adds.

Has it ever happened to you that the other person says exactly the thing that you have been thinking of, and at that very moment? True friends mostly know it all. And I like Sheen, just for that!

'I will see.' I tell her, just to draw out that I-don't-give-a-shit look on her face.

Alara reminds me of Elisha. While there's hardly a chance that they would be related, I must check on her just to be sure. The crowd goes mad as she steps down the stage, and I realize that another star is born, right here at Ricky's.

Now it's Aarav who has to perform. I know this champ will rule the stage.

'Aarav, go for it!' I scream as he looks stupefied on stage. After a long pause, almost three minutes, he starts:

Hi

I am Aarav.

Sad, depressed, and a comic. I know ironic. Or is it? I don't know.

So I am recently single. It's hard. I have started hating every couple around me. And the rock bottom of the problem is not that you are single. You hit rock bottom when you find out that even fucking Ramesh has a girlfriend now. Ramesh has one. Ramesh. You know Ramesh? He asks the audience.

A girl from the audience replies no.

See, that is how unremarkable Ramesh is. Fucking Ramesh from accounts.

Ah . . .

So we broke up six months ago. By we, I mean SHE decided that it is not working anymore between US.

Ah . . .

I really loved her. I really do love her. Do not know why. I hate her. I hate that her one smile can make your day. I hate that she brings joy to people around her. WITH JUST A SMILE. Do you know how long I had to hone my skills to be this good. And I am not even good. That bitch.

I am scared. I am scared shitless.

I lost the only good thing in my life, Tara. I am contemplating leaving my job.

I am thinking of moving.

I am most probably depressed.

And somehow that's not even the worst thing in my life currently. He laughs nervously.

The worst thing is, I don't know how to date. Like, not anymore. I never knew.

We met, we were friends and became lovers.

Lover. What a fucking cheesy word, lovers.

It should be losers. He laughs hysterically. That's my time folks.

I snatch the mic from Aarav as I walk up the stage. In a most disgusting tone I ask him to get lost. Sometimes it gets on my nerves how he is not able to be on stage without mentioning Tara.

I don't want him to cry over her for years like I did for Elisha.

I clear my throat and address a silent audience: 'The best part of me, which at least I adore the most, is that I was willing to adapt and learn. My encounters with people, all through my life, were my best teachers. I do not believe in the conservative education protocols. I believed that learning comes from doing and the rest from gathering wisdom gained by others through their own personal experiences through their lives. What was the biggest failure of my life two years back doesn't matter anymore. Neither do any of those achievements. Just believe in time. It cures the largest of wounds. You can take back something positive from even the most negative experiences or crib even while experiencing the most amazing things. Life is how you look at it and how you make it. There's no absolute. Play the goddamn music.'

I get off the stage, walk up to Aarav and snap, 'Don't want to see you here again!'

'I am not coming back. Maybe I don't have it in me. And no matter how hard I practise, I can't get past the thoughts of Tara.'

'We all have our means of release. Some of us like to run, some of us play sports, some of us dance our hurt out, some of us sing it out aloud, while the rest of us choose to cry. There's nothing wrong about crying, once in a while. You must cry. Vulnerability is your strength. But to cry over and over will not lead you anywhere. Rather, if you feel joy, find your release. If you feel hurt, find your release. You can't burden your people with the task of making you feel good about yourself all the time. At times, you must choose an activity that liberates your mind from the pain. And trust me, we all might have different methods of release, but we all have one for sure. I want this stage to be your method of release. Understand?'

I pick a corner and gulp my eighth drink of the day. Dejected and clueless, Aarav sits next to me.

Alara drags a chair to sit with us. She points to an old photograph of hers, 'This is me, singing at the age of nine. Never have I ever cared about who's watching! I sing, in joy and in pain. When in pain, I sing louder, clearer! It's not about reaching out to someone else. It's about talking to my own soul. I heal. I mostly heal after that!'

'He stills needs lots of practising and brushing up. It is definitely not his best. But I am sure that the best is yet to come. Let him take his time.'

'You remind me of someone,' I say as I look into Alara's eyes.

'Should I be concerned?' she smiles at me. That smile! That smile in particular reminds me of Elisha, and her songs, innocence.

'Who all have been your musical influences?' I ask.

'Not many. Madonna, Shakira, Avril, these are the ones that I have grown up watching,' she replies.

'Your style isn't mainstream, it's not like one of those pop singers. It's hard to believe that you're telling the right thing.'

'Why would I lie?' she smiles with confidence.

And, yes! Why would she lie? My drinks get the better of me sometimes. But there's something really strange about her.

'What brings you here?'

'I need to write new songs. Travel is the best way they say.' Elisha was not particularly good at handling criticism, I remember. 'Your voice is perfect, but it feels like something is missing.'

'Something? As in? I did not get you?' she retorts in surprise, her voice louder than usual.

'While playing with one instrument one should be prepared. Focus on more original songs, as that is the spirit of Ricky's Beach Shack. You may come down here during the day and practice with Shiva. Shiva plays the guitar for us.'

'Okay.'

'What is it that sets some journeys apart from the others?' I ask, curious to see who answers first, and of course better! That's one of the tricks I learnt from my mother.

Alara volunteers, 'All of us have the traits of a hero within us, and ideally all of us are heroes. Each one of us experiences the negative emotion of fear at some point in our lives, just like the heroes whose journeys we're celebrating. What makes a difference is to make a move or take an action to overcome it.'

Aarav quips, 'I don't believe that all of us become heroes, but it is important to set out on the journey of a hero.'

'So, what are you waiting for?' Alara and I say in unison. Thereafter, we laugh at the coincidence.

'Does she remind you of Elisha?' Aarav breaks the silence. He looks at Alara and continues, 'I hope not.

Otherwise, your weekend employment is cancelled. He hates her.'

'Who is she?' Alara replies.

'She can't remind me of Elisha. Her voice is perfect but songs lack the depth of emotions and the beautiful stories that Elisha told through her music,' I say.

'My music teacher told me to write down what I feel during sleepless nights. It will help me heal. That's what I do! It's hurting to know that you feel I am not good enough.'

'If you plan to do something, you have to be the best at it. You will survive being mediocre, but it is a whole other ball game to go beyond that. Expecting you to be better next week.' Her face turns visibly red. She must assume that she's the best, but she isn't. I have certainly seen the best and she is not it.

'Hmm,' she replies.

'It is not at all about what you achieve or where you reach. It is about doing what you love to do. And giving your 100 per cent to it. For instance, a music teacher and a rock star both love music.'

I am sure Aarav and Alara would come better prepared for the next performance. These kids need to be told. I have faith that they can do much better. Your relationship with your trainer is bittersweet but it is worth it.

Life's about making the most of your present to build a better future and not shed tears in the name of the past! Everyone has had their share of tragedies, but it's time to pat yourself on your back and move on.

Aarav is a good lad. I know he has the potential to make the world laugh like crazy. He needs to get serious and believe in himself. I see my past broken self in him. I'll try my best to let his dreams come true and help him take the path I myself did not.

You're that one person who is going to stay with you till the end. Make sure that you love this person first and then spread the love. A lot of people often ask me, 'How do I spread so much love, life and laughter?' It is simply because I love myself.

LOOKING FOR YOU

Alara

Sunday, 3 November 2019
Maria's PG for Working Women
Canacona
Goa, India

'It is in the moments when we lose ourselves,
our sanity, that we actually feel alive.'

Yesterday, I felt so tempted to enquire about mom but the moment Aarav told me about what Ricky feels about her, I held back from asking anything in particular. Last night was magical. I've got to write and perform a new song this week. I need to win over Ricky if I want him to tell me more about my mom.

As I am lost in thought, the reception guy calls me.

'Parvathi is here to see you. You can come down to the reception,' he says.

'What's up?'

'All good.'

'Ready to go for house hunting?'

'Yeah!'

'By the way, I think I know the best place for you. You will like it there. We're visiting three PGs in the neighbourhood, but I'm sure you will finalize the first one.'

'Let's see!'

We walk by the Palolem Beach Road for about a kilometre to reach a 2-storey Portuguese construction on top of a rock formation. It is slightly secluded from the more commercial places around.

'I like it already,' I assure Parvathi.

We reach the building that feels at least thirty years old. An old lady sits at the porch basking in the sun. A young lady, probably the old lady's nurse, walks up to us. 'Are you here to check out the room?' A white Pomeranian dog accompanies her. 'Lucky, keep sitting,' she instructs. Lucky jumps and licks us in joy, ignoring her commands.

'Yes, I am Parvathi. And she is Alara. She is the tenant.'

'Namaste, I am Madhuri,' she greets and leads us to the top floor. She introduces the old lady as Maria, the owner of the PG. I shake hands with her. They are as soft as freshly churned butter from the centrifuge. She seems paralyzed waist down as Madhuri helps her with the wheelchair. Maria seems to be of Portuguese descent for sure. I can tell from her face.

The room is a tiny refuge constructed of grey stones. It has a small terrace attached to it. It overlooks the Arabian Sea. Although it is not very big, it is just perfect to accommodate me. And Parvathi was quite right when she presumed that I would take this place.

'How much will it be?'

'You're planning to stay until the New Years? That's what Parvathi told me over the phone call.'

'Yes!'

'We generally do not let out our rooms for less than six months. But this penthouse has been vacant for a long time. Nobody wants to stay so far cut-off from the city centre. So, we've decided to let you have it at 30,000 rupees for two months. You have to pay 50 per cent in advance,' she says mechanically. It seems like Maria does not speak much and has trained Madhuri to look after her and the property.

'I'm moving in today,' I reply with a smile.

I head back to the hotel and Parvathi helps me do up my new place. '*Didi*, write as your heart desires on this desk. I am sure you will touch a million souls,' she says and walks out.

She tells me that she has to pick her mother up from a nearby orphanage where she works as a nurse.

I hit the beach for the very first time since I have arrived. As I jump and dance all on my own, I feel so liberated as I can live like Ramy for two months. I have watched it in the movies for so long, but this feels pretty real now. I am at a place where I can be who I wish to be without adhering to the norms of the society. Splashing around in the water like the birds and animals from the jungle, singing and shouting out loud, contemplating and writing my next song, running endlessly along the shore, trekking up the cliffs nearby. Yes, this is my home. In the wilderness, don't let your phone ring, only your heart sing!

Like Ramy says on his blog *on the open road*: The world is our home. It is delusional to call your apartment home. Even worse, to stick to the same place all through your lives. If you've found love, happiness, or togetherness somewhere, you've certainly found a home.

Relax. Calm down. Meditate. Your mind needs cleansing just like your body. When you travel, make sure that you cleanse your mind and soul in the embrace of nature, flowing water preferably. The sound of water acts like a healer. Always take some time out to spend with yourself and heal. I am cleansing myself in the Arabian Sea, literally. The water is clear as crystal and as green and glittery as emerald, and I'm sure it has taken a journey traversing ages, universes. What if a part of it has touched my mother too.

I feel as if I was a sea of madness, bubbling to break free. As I danced by the shore, I finally did! It is in the moments when we lose ourselves, our sanity, that we actually feel alive.

In the evening I walk to the small restaurant-cum-mess downstairs for dinner. A few girls are sitting here and there, chatting about everything from the current government to boyfriends. Madhuri enters the place and, as usual, she is with Maria.

Maria, while seated on her wheelchair, gestures at me with her index finger to come closer. I follow her command. She then gestures at Madhuri to get her a pen maybe. In no time she hands her a diary and a pen. She trembles as she scribbles, 'Who is she?'

Madhuri tells her that I am the new tenant who has moved in today. She then whispers in my ears, 'Don't worry! She is too old. She has Alzheimer's. She forgets too often. Go, get your plate.'

Next morning, as I am practising songs on my terrace, someone rings my room's bell. I open to see that Madhuri and Maria are my guests.

'She needs to sit in the sun every day for an hour. I hope you will not mind. We have only one terrace. She likes the view from here.'

'Oh sure! Why not?'

Madhuri leaves Maria with a diary and a pen. She probably has some chores to finish off downstairs. I continue to practise. Lucky sits next to Maria.

I set my guitar and sing,

Heaven is white
only in fiction.
It is certainly blue
and green in reality.
What's your drug?
Mine is the sea, rains.

What's your drug?
Or the mountains.

Maria closes her eyes as she rests in her wheelchair. She is facing the sky, with her eyes closed. It feels as if she is listening to my song.

I tell Maria, 'I would like to stay near the sea for the rest of my life.' Why did I say that? 'I love the ocean, any form of it, any view of it, the sound of it. It soothes me and relaxes my soul. It makes me feel that I am alive.'

She smiles but doesn't reply. I assume that she might use her pen to write something, but she does not do that either. Helpless, as I had not spoken to anyone since morning, I continue to sing and take down the music notes in my diary.

A few minutes later, she picks up the pen and draws a heart.

'My songs are wonderful?' I ask as my face lights up like an LED bulb.

She shakes her head in a 'no'.

'My songs remind you of love?' I ask again. She shakes her head again!

She scribbles, 'You sing from the heart.'

'Thank you!'

'You remind me of someone,' she whispers in a broken voice. I smile at her. Maybe most Goans feel so as they might see a reflection of my mother in me.

This also breaks my suspicion that Maria can't speak. She can, but she chooses not to.

'Who?'

'I don't remember,' she replies.

Madhuri returns and escorts her back for lunch. I continue to practise. Later, I place the new song in the box. This box is one of the most valuable things I have, like a treasure. While a lot of people evaluate things in money, does it ever occur to you that most of those things are replaceable. However, only the irreplaceable things in our life can never be bought with any amount of money.

Then, I make friends with Akkriti, a prostitute who fled from Mumbai where she was sold for trade and who now works at a library nearby. Her story is no short of an inspirational film. The best part of her that I admire is that she chooses to smile.

I couldn't ever understand what ugly meant? Maybe, ugly is only when we're angry, jealous, or depressed—as it just reflects from our face and we can't help but make people sad in our presence. But when we're happy, full of enthusiasm and love, we just radiate that positivity and spread smiles wherever we go. Maybe, it's not about being beautiful or ugly. Maybe, it's just about being happy or sad. And yes, there would be times when you would be sad, but the moment you decide to smile again, you're beautiful again, you're beautiful always.

As promised, Parvathi comes to see me post sunset. A few minutes later, we lie next to each other beneath a full moon as we gaze at the endless night sky that is absorbed in the cold breeze from the sea and the water twinkling from the lights of the shacks.

'Ricky feels I am not good enough yet!'

'Ricky is a retired psycho. I had warned you. I should not have taken you to Ricky's.'

'Look up towards the sky. Infinite, isn't it?'

'Look within and you'll realize you're infinite too,' she smiles with belief.

Her faith in me urges me to share my sweet little secret with her. 'Elisha is my mother.'

Her eyes open wide in amazement. She stays silent for a while and says, 'Are you out of your mind? If that's true, you must tell everyone and become a superstar.'

'Someday, I will. Not now. I want to keep away from the media glare. I wish to know more about my mother. That's my goal. Especially, what happened to her. Dad told me that they never found her body. I feel she must be living under an alternate identity, you know!'

'I am with you in this journey. Consider me as your closest confidant. I will help you.'

'Will I be able to find her? Ever?'

'Walking away from anything in life is easy. But to stay resolute, to hold on, to wait for the sunrise is difficult. You're doing just that!'

'Do you have any friends here?'

'Not really, most of them left to pursue higher education. My family has financial constraints. I like to assist my mother at the orphanage. I will also join as a nurse there.'

'Boyfriend?'

'I don't want a guy to look at me as an object of lust. I want the same feelings of trust, care, and security from a guy that he holds for his sister or mom. Is that too much to ask for? Most guys I met misconstrued my search for love as a search for lust. I don't want that! How about you?'

'I haven't dated anyone. I'm single.'

'Hard to believe that as you're from Prague. May I ask why?'

'I am close to my guitar. People often fail to meet your expectations. Unfulfilled expectations lead to unfulfilled relationships. One such relationship was that of my parents.'

'You might find love in Goa then!' she winks.

'The ocean is the man of my dreams, I surrender myself to his depth, he lets me loose at the seams. I indulge in this endless play, until the sun calls it a day,' I compose and sing these lines in the moment.

'Looks like the singer is at work!'

'Yes! Yes! Yes!'

We spend the next 2-3 hours chatting away about everything from beaches to travel to life to career to dreams. We bid goodbye to each other with a promise of meeting again the next morning.

No amount of words can ever express the bond that is friendship. After telling my secret to her, I am already feeling better. Friendship is the best medicine.

I don't have a dream home. I never had a clear picture of what it looks like. It could be in a village by the farms, or by the ocean, or in the embrace of green blue hills, or simply in the suburbs of some city. It just doesn't matter. But I do have a clear picture of what my dream home looks like. It has to be a place where everyone loves each other, moreover, accepts each other for the way they are, allows each other to be the free-spirited souls they are, rather than constraining them in the shackles of society, where they are free from prejudice, command, and bigotry. Where the only 'wrong' is to not love each other and the only 'right' is to be one's true self. No lies. No fear. Absolutely no quarrels. If we are all made up of stardust, the universe is our home and confining our beliefs to a society is often misleading.

THE FIRE WITHIN YOU

Aarav

Saturday, 9 November 2019
Carnival Cafe and Bar
Koregaon Park
Pune, India

'They try to break me. Again and again. I don't
give up, I rise, again and again.'

I wake up to a notification of 10 rupees being split on *Splitwise*. My flat-mate Jeswant is a crazy asshole. He was once orgasming in public over a phone call to satisfy his stupid girlfriend who wouldn't stop demanding that he does that immediately. That's the level of crazy we're talking about. What's more? He's a miser too! While I have so many reasons to move to Goa, getting out of this rat-hole is a primary one.

'All the best!' Uncle Ricky calls me up at 8 AM in the morning.

'Thank you!'

'I am sure you will rock.'

'I feel so too!'

'Are you not upset about coming to Ricky's tonight?'

'I am more upset about not seeing Alara.'

'I'm glad you're taking interest. They say only a new girl can make you forget the old one.'

'Why could you not move on then? You've been dating so many new girls!'

'Elisha was not like a movie with a defined beginning and end. She was more like her songs which can be experienced by each one in a different way, going back to a different time in their lives. I couldn't find another like her,' says Uncle Ricky, the helpless romantic.

'I have work,' I hang up on him.

Alara feels like my Elisha! The other day, Alara told me to write about almost anything that I feel. I used to do it earlier as well, but now I am much more sincere. I don't want to let anyone down during my next performance.

I scribble in my diary:

Dear future me,
You were their shadow until the day
You looked into the window
And discovered the warrior within.

I book an *Uber Pool* to office. Though Saturdays are usually off for me, we have an important client deal to close today. If everything works fine, Akshaye's temperament and my monthly bonus will be sorted. Papa's retirement is due and I will be able to throw a lavish party. My relatives wouldn't have witnessed something half as good as it. It will be enough fodder for the donkeys to keep talking for a year. They might not focus as much on my career decisions then.

Seated with me in the *Uber Pool* are two middle-aged aunties who are en route to a shopping mall. They request our driver to drop them off first.

'Aarav's drop is showing first. I can't change the navigation route,' he tries to make them understand.

They let out a resigned sigh, not convinced of the driver's moves.

I take my diary out and scribble:

When people book Uber Pool, they look at others with a mental block that why the fuck are they even here in the first place. If they have so much money, why can't they get themselves an exclusive ride?

I make it to the office just in time. I press the elevator button a couple of times only to realize that none of the three are working!

'What happens when the lift at your 11-floor building does not work?' snaps Akshaye as he reaches 5 minutes after me.

'You get to know how fit you are!' I say almost as an impulse.

'Your jokes are getting better!'

'I'm performing in Pune tonight.'

'I know.'

But Akshaye isn't the kind who would look up shows on *BookMyShow*.

'How?'

'Ricky asked me to go watch you perform!'

'Oh! Uncle Ricky.'

'Get ready for the meeting. I will be back in a while.'

The month I joined HSBC, Akshaye had sponsored a formal dinner for us on account of his promotion. The team was invited to Colorin, the restaurant I was mentioning the other day. I heard one of the team members say, 'I don't want to go back to the same old cubicle. I want to start a company.' I moved towards him with a fancy of a child towards balloons. He was speaking with four other teammates. I stood there to start a conversation as he declared, 'Start-ups are all the rage now. They are encompassing the Indian landscape like nothing has ever before. Not that companies did not exist before. They did. But it is different now!' Everyone, including me, nodded.

I had interrupted to catch his attention, 'Hello, Shikhar! You must be aware, I am Aarav. We sit next to each other but haven't spoken yet. That is kind of weird.'

He quipped, 'I am apprehensive about starting a conversation with non-IITians. I believe there is nothing in common to talk about.'

I replied, 'Try me then,' as I did not approve of such prejudice. He said, 'Chill! Don't get mad at me.'

We laughed. This is how it all started. This is how I met Shikhar.

Shikhar and I are the interns in Akshaye's team. Shikhar greets me in the lobby. There's still half an hour to go before the meeting.

'When are your placements starting? Is it laid back like every other thing in Goa?' he smiles.

'January. Have you made up your mind?'

'Throughout the interviews for campus placements I have been lying to my potential employers. Those lies have gotten me this far but refuse to take me any further. I need to start my venture. My potential co-founders are in place.'

'All from your college?'

'Not really. One is from IIT. The other one we found on an angel network site.'

'Happy to see the shift in your mindset.'

'You aren't an IITian, Aarav, but you're really talented. You've changed my mindset. Also, I am happy to see you grow as a stand-up comic. What are your plans?'

'The probability of getting what we want during the placements is bleak. We're made to apply to every company. The funniest part is, we map our skills to the profile being offered and not hunt for the profile that matches our skills.'

'It happens back in IIT too!' We share a sarcastic laugh.

'My parents want me to have a job. Stand-up comedy is part-time. My dad is retiring soon, you know!'

'Maybe you can write a script on the plight of middle-class Indians. So many people will be able to relate to it. Even I can.'

'That is a good idea, bro! By the way I am performing for the first time in Pune. Join me tonight.'

'Of course, brother! Will be there. Share the details on *WhatsApp*.'

Shikhar always tells me, 'The world knows who you want to become. You know who you want to become. Yet, every day, you don't come home to your own self.'

I finish the meeting and secure my share for throwing my father a party. I then rush to Carnival. With jitters down my spine and a racing heart I tell myself that I will rock tonight.

On reaching, a volunteer guides me to the green room. I find three other stand-ups sitting there as I enter. They aren't really speaking to each other. Sandeep and Ankush know each other, while Ruchi, the only woman stand-up, is being ignored on purpose. They give a cold response to my over-enthusiastic hellos.

'You go first,' the volunteer tells me, 'next is yours,' he tells Ruchi, 'then you,' he points to Ankush. We nod. 'You're the showstopper,' he tells Sandeep.

Sandeep says to the volunteer, 'The coffee tastes like shit. Can you get me some warm water, please?'

'Okay,' he nods and leaves.

Sandeep tells Ankush, 'These young stand-ups, I tell you. They're full of shit. There's no class. They talk about stereotypes. No pun. No sarcasm.'

'They aren't even punctual,' Ankush adds.

Ruchi, meanwhile, is busy rehearsing. I take my diary out and scribble:

> *They try to break me.*
> *Again and again.*
> *I don't give up, I rise,*
> *again and again.*

As the light over the audience dims and a spotlight moves over me, I am reminded of Alara, not Tara. It feels as if she is standing in the crowd and is asking me to give my best. It is comforting in a good way. I smile, then I start:

Any lazy people in the crowd?

The crowd goes 'wohooo' and almost 20 people raise their hands.

Oh. Ugh . . .You guys have too much energy to be called lazy. Shame on you. You disgust me. Booo booo. Haha.

Shame! (There is a sound of a gong behind me.) *Shame!*

(The gong sounds again.)

Shame! (And again.)

Hehehe.

I am legitimately lazy. I can even get that notarized. I don't work or even move if it's not important. I would not have come here if I hadn't lost a toss to Uncle Ricky. Cheers to him, he is my mentor. The crowd breaks into whispers.

I also do that flower thing people do in movies. He loves me, he loves me not. But mine, instead, is: should I move today, should I not? I giggle.

This is not even a phase of life. It's just me. Like in college, I could have topped my Math classes. But I got straight Cs. Because I wrote exactly enough to pass and not a sentence more.

I could have been some big shot corporate suit by now. But that's too much work. Like fuck that, I would prefer being poor but satisfied.

I love being single too. This statement is the Gayatri Mantra of all single people. It's just dope. No one to nag. No one sitting on your ass all the time. My tone suddenly takes a condescending turn. *Do this. Don't do that. You have done that wrong. It should have been this way. No, you can't have that much candy. No you cannot deep fry cheese-dipped extra-cheese cheese burger. What are you, a 12-year-old?*

Life is too short. And I want to be a 12-year-old. Even when my schoolteachers asked me what I wanted to be when I grow old, any guesses? I said, a-12 year-old.

Laughter erupts through the crowd. *She wasn't amused. She thought I wanted to HAVE a 12-year-old . . . which I now think is a dope idea. I think I should adopt a kid. It would be like getting an intern for life. For life, I say. It's like free labour. I have to provide him what, the basic necessities. He would clean the house, do the dishes. He would be like my personal Cinderella who would never find her prince.*

What? Hahaha. He would be grateful that I saved him from the hole I picked him up from. The abortion, I mean, adoption clinic. I don't know where they come from.

It's just improv at the moment. Hmm . . . free labour. He would do every shitty thing I don't like to do. He would be so good for living out my bitching philosophy.

You don't really have to do anything. And if you do, make the orphan do it.

I can see a few of you are starting to turn on me. And this makes me realize, I really wouldn't like to be quoted on what I just said. Really. It might be funny but it's really dark, even for me.

I can just see tomorrow's headline 'INSENSITIVE COMIC OFFENDS ORPHANS' and the nation wants an apology from the buffoon who thinks it's okay to make fun of orphans, and after that I should leave my country.

End of story, but not the discussion.

I have started watching DD as I can not stand the poison, the hate, and the opinion eccentric regular news. DD is still full-on facts. I believe if news is interesting, it's flawed and doctored. I started a hashtag for that: MAKE NEWS BORING AGAIN. News is just bombarded on us with no context now. Headlines go like: Pakistan is trying to invade India; up next, opposition caught in a corruption scandal; up next, onion prices are at 150 per kilo; up next, was Karina in Ibiza with Ranbeer; and then there is a genocide happening in Thailand.

And you be like, honestly, was the story about onions even important?

Who the fuck cares about onions, tell me what's happening in Ibiza.

To make matters even more fun, it's all sponsored by penis enhancement pills which actually makes you impotent. And somehow, we think we live in the golden age of information and television.

Think. Think. Think. That's my time folks.

I receive a round of laughter and applause, followed by people standing up as they continue to clap. It turns out to be my best performance so far. I place a hand on my beating heart and tell myself that I have a long way to go!

I walk down to see Akshaye and Shikhar. Akshaye is accompanied by his wife Urmila.

Urmila says, 'Hello, Aarav! You've got some real talent. What are you doing working at a bank?' Akshaye passes a sly smile to her.

'Boss is very encouraging of my stand-up acts. It's my family that wants me to be at the bank.'

Shikhar adds, 'The problem with the world is that they want to see the results too soon. Good things take time to work, so sit back, relax, and have faith.'

Akshaye laughs, 'When life hits you hard, you can always hit back harder.'

I look at the other stand-ups before leaving and I know that I don't want to be one of them. The idea is to build and nurture a community that cares, respects, and loves each one. We are not here to fight or compete against each other. We must learn to grow as a community, help others to achieve goals. I want to be like Uncle Ricky in a lot of ways. I just can't wait to tell Uncle Ricky about today.

OUR SECRET HIDEAWAY—I

Ricky

Friday, 24 November 2019
Canacona Island
Goa, India

'A bond will form in a place but a bond will rest in time.'

'May I come in?' someone whispers in a feeble voice. It's still 5 AM and we don't expect guests during this time. Harinder and I are usually the only ones awake at this odd hour as we expect some food and alcohol delivery to some huts. But Harinder has gone back to his village in Punjab. I turn only to recognize a dark silhouette of a woman standing at the entrance of Ricky's. Since the lights aren't turned on, it is only the feeble light from the sun at dawn that can help me try to recognize who it is. I move in the direction of the mysterious woman.

'Elisha,' I whisper with equal parts surprise and disgust. My feet go numb.

'Hello, Ricky. I really miss you.'

'You have not aged a bit. That's miraculous.'

'But you look like a retired psycho sailor, just like I had imagined.'

'I can't believe that you're standing here right in front of me. Where have you been? All these years?'

I stand on the other side of the door, looking straight into her eyes. She does not answer me. Rather, she moves in the opposite direction. I long to kiss her passionately, but only gather an uncomfortable silence that stretches up to miles. The veil of conscience holds me back this time, like every other time.

Soon, she has left the gate and starts to move towards the side of the beach that leads to the Canacona Island, separated by a narrow backwater formation from Palolem Beach. It's the same island where we used to go years back and discuss everything, like the best of friends do.

It reminds me of the question Elisha would always ask me. 'If a wish of yours could come true, what would it be?'

'If I were granted a wish, just one, I would time travel and be an explorer in the 18th century. Someone like Captain Picault who extensively explored the Seychelles and eventually made it accessible to all the nomads, travellers, and explorers of the 21st century!'

'And you?' I would ask.

'I would want a daughter like myself who is a singer,' she would say.

She doesn't seem to stop. I hesitantly ask her, 'How is Mr. Czech?' She doesn't reply. I keep moving towards her.

Canacona Island is not inhabited by humans. The woods at dawn seem so dark, and there is ultimate silence, miles away from all the commotion. We start to wander along a solitary path, only to encounter an abandoned boat. A perfect place isn't a myth. You will always find it in the middle of nowhere.

She stops by the end of the island, I stand beside her. There's nothing to be seen except for the horizon that separates the sea from the sky.

It is one of those moments in which you feel bliss in simply existing, looking at the sky through the net-like canopy of trees. Sky is hope. Sky is possibilities. Sky is perspective. You only see it as far as it is visible, but that does not mean that there is nothing beyond. Sailing on ships, I would often do that. Youngsters hooked to mobile phones will never know the pleasure.

'Why is it so hard to fall out of love?' I ask her, hopelessly. She never asked me to stay. I never told her I would leave.

Words left unsaid are the hardest to live with. But today is a chance to talk about it.

'Loving someone is a decision that we make. You can choose to love someone else.'

'You don't choose to fall in love with someone, neither do you choose to fall out of it. If it was as simple as taking a decision, are all these statements like 'I fell in love', 'it was love at first sight', 'I could not help but fall in love', 'love just happens' bullshit? Void?'

'We can try. Sometimes, that's all we can do,' she says as she holds my hand and continues, 'Why didn't you ever say it?'

I feel a spark of lightning travel down my body. If I had said I love you, my life would have become much easier, my sufferings might have mitigated and I would have achieved my ultimate destiny which lies in your arms, away from tears, but I feared that the magic which prevails in the air marking your presence and which energizes my senses would also be lost. The sound of silence strikes a chord deep down under, where neither the tears of rain reach nor the thunder.

'I never wanted to lose you!'

'I left you,' she says with equal parts sorrow and regret. This whole concept of time is so messed up. The moment when you meet someone determines everything. She might never have felt this when we were together. She must have realized it after I left.

I assert, 'It is always one person who decides to move on in a relationship.'

'Yes. And why did you not move on?'

'Did not feel the need to. If we hadn't gotten married, we might have broken up. If we had, we might have gotten divorced. And even if we had decided to stay together forever, one of us would have died before the other. But you are mine today. This today is forever. Nothing means forever like the tiny moments in which we live a lifetime. I'm happy in this momentary bond. I have felt forever so many times.'

'Is one-sided love a bond?'

'Yes. Some people keep loving without getting anything in return. Some people keep loving getting a lot of hatred and disrespect in return. Love is a messed up thing. Relationships are messy, aren't they?'

'Can a bond become bondage?'

'Not for me. It has helped me become a better version of me. Vulnerability is my strength. Intimacy impacts individuality. You can't do this. That. I am free from all that nonsense.'

Fit in or fly away. I choose the latter.

'Strength and weakness are not separate from each other. What is strength today could be a weakness on some other occasion, for some other person.'

'I can never win an argument with you.' I laugh out loud.

'I love that,' she says.

'And him,' I add as I shrug and whisper underneath my breath. 'I can never be him. You can never be mine. But, I can still be myself, and there is nothing better to be.'

'Wake up, Ricky!' I hear someone shouting in the background. I turn back and the voice gets louder, but there is no one to be seen. Then, I see Sheen. She's panting and running towards me. 'Ricky, you will be the death of me. Why are you so careless and selfish?'

In a moment I realize that I am wide awake from a dream and not standing but lying on the shore. The place is just about the same, except there's no Elisha to be seen.

It is all within us. The monster and the God. The truth and the lies. Dreams and reality.

'How did I get here?' I ask, clueless and dejected.

'That's a question I should be asking. Isn't it?'

'I can't feel my legs. I am too intoxicated.'

'Ricky! Grow up. What if it were high tide? You would have been swept away by the waves. I can't afford to lose you.'

'Don't be worried about me. I don't deserve so much. Ricky's is yours after I die,' I laugh as I press my hands against my stomach.

'You deserve that, and much more. I love you.' She helps me get up by offering me a helping hand. Sheen has taught me so much. In relationships, one has to be transparent and reflecting like water. Love back, give back, don't only expect things from other people.

I laugh hysterically at my situation, my dream, my life, which is no short of an artwork.

'How can you be so happy all the time?' Sheen wonders.

'Happiness comes in various shades, shapes, and forms. Happiness is omnipresent. Happiness comes from within. All you have to do is decide to be happy.'

'What about the pain that we feel?'

'Pain is temporary. It heals after a while. Your life is a mixed bag of emotions. Cherish them all.'

As we keep moving along the beach, I come across a beautiful shell. I pick it up and adjust it on my finger. After sailing for so long, I did fall in love again, but with the sea. This bond feels like it would last an eternity. It never fades, just gets stronger with every passing day. This shell-like ring on my finger is just a token for you to see. What I feel is something I may never be able to express in words.

Meditation for me is floating free in the ocean, shallow or deep, Indian or Mediterranean, blue or green, it simply does not matter. Ocean heals me in ways nothing ever has or ever will. Search for that one thing in life that gives you immense happiness and keep going back to it. It may not necessarily be human. It's this bond that brings me to Canacona Island, all on my own, often.

I form a bond with everything. I feel that God has placed beauty and love all around us; in the tiniest of pebbles, sand, grass (golden or green), in the mountains, in the snow, in the dolphins and the horses, in the quest for the meaning of life. Now you might think that I am saying this because I am in Goa—a supposed heaven on earth, and so it makes sense for me to say that. But I formed bonds back on the ship too, back in time too.

Have you ever felt pain while abandoning an apartment and moving to another? Yes, I have and so have you.

Have you ever cried for hours because someone too close to you passed away? Of course you have.

Have you ever loved knowing that the other person doesn't love you? Yes!

We all form bonds. Rather, it's only human to form bonds, ephemeral or forever. And you must find peace in your capacity to make deep and fulfilling bonds with everything around you.

The thing you've come to form a bond with will not be by your side forever. Neither will you. Again, that's nature—ever changing yet magnificent. But the love that you'll receive and give back will last forever.

Will bonds hurt? Yes, they will. But bonds will heal you too.

A bond will form in a place, but a bond will rest in time. Why do we feel so strongly for some things in life? Some experiences? Some people? I don't have an answer and that's when I know I have found a soulmate. It is love beyond imagination. My feelings are as deep and unfathomable as the depth of the sea.

The sea has taught me so much that I now look up to it as my mentor, my family. The waves taught me to be consistent in my efforts. They are proof that the hardest of rocks become sand when the waves don't give up. The sea has helped me discover the most beautiful of species and the most precious of rock matter.

I still remember my days back on an island in the southern Indian Ocean when afternoons would mean playing with the starfish and jellyfish that would float by my side! The sea is the love of my life, and yes, it is okay to fall in love with nature, and I know that it will keep calling me and teaching me the best of lessons. Sometimes I discover things and sometimes I just discover myself with every minute I spend by the sea.

Sheen and I take a walk back to the shack, crossing the backwaters. It's still shallow and can be crossed on foot. I head back to my room to take a nap.

'You are mad,' Sheen says as she leaves the room.

'You must be double mad to fall in love with a mad person.'

'Maybe, yes!'

'Madness is a crucial part of our lives. Take a man and add some madness to him. Now, he chirps, sings, laughs, jumps and does everything that most common people will consider craziness. But who is really crazy? The one who jumps and dances and chirps all over the scene, spreading love and positivity, or the one who sits in the corner imagining what went wrong that he can no longer do what this other person is doing?'

'Sleep well, Ricky!'

I am not proud of risking my life and bothering Sheen, but I'm happy to have spoken to Elisha after such a long time. Let me tell you what exactly triggered this. Three days back, Alara had come to me. It is her fault.

She rekindled the spark in me. She made me believe that Elisha might still be alive. While I had dragged her out of Ricky's that very day, I feel I should call her up and help her find Elisha. If there's the slightest of truth in it, I am willing to take a chance. You know why? Because you always want to give one last chance to the people you love. I pick up the landline placed on my bedside and dial Maria's.

'Hello.'

'Yes. Madhuri from Maria's PG.'

'Can I speak with Alara?'

'Yes!' After a moment, 'Hi,' says Alara.

'This Sunday, we are going to your mother's school.'

'Thank you! I knew you would call me. My happiness knows no bounds Uncle Ricky.'

'Be on time!' I say as I hang up.

Elisha's words from my dream, 'I love that', spin in my head like she had said I love you. I re-hear and relive them a zillion times. The feeling? I can't exactly put it into words.

Drinking alone is not the best feeling to have. It feels like you seek some company which is long lost, almost not there. You want to be with them, but somehow they are too far away, almost oblivious. But then, you see them, it is all you ever wanted. It is the best and the worst feeling in the world. Then you ask yourself, should you be happy or should you be happy at all?

Should you be happy that you've finally found them or should you be sad that there would be times when, no matter how hard you try, you won't be able to find them? So, at this moment, I should have been happy. I should have been happy because what I wanted had just happened, right in front of my eyes, right where I wanted it to be, right how I wanted it to be.

Life, like love, can get confusing at times. We look for answers in black and white but return home with shades of grey.

SLEEPLESS IN HOPE

Alara

Sunday, 1 December 2019
Saint Paul's Higher Secondary School
Goa, India

'It is not going to be easy; you will need a
release at some point in your life. The choice
between tears and sweat will make all the
difference.'

This week has been a crazy ride. By the way, I succeeded in completing and performing another song for the album last night. Sunday, yes, the day has arrived when Uncle Ricky is finally taking me to the school.

It is like one of the days when you can't sleep for the anxiety of not waking up on time the next day. I am wide awake before even the sun has come up, looking at the clock as each second passes by. As I get ready and I am about to leave at 8 AM sharp, Akkriti, another occupant of the PG who I have befriended, knocks at my door.

'It's a little cold during the nights now,' she says.

'Yeah! When you're near the sand you feel the heat during the day and cold during the night.'

'Actually, I need your help. I feel a little scared going to the store room alone. And I can't sleep because the blanket in my room is worthless. Mine is in the trolley I have kept there.'

'Sure, why not? Let us go and get it together.'

As she unpacks her stuff to get her blanket out, I roll my eyes to take in every corner of the room and scan through all the unattended and old things lying around. My gaze falls upon a chest of drawers on which an old chart paper is placed with 'Lost and Found' hand-written on it. I feel instantly attracted to it and move towards it.

I scan through the drawers one by one. I stumble upon a folder labelled Room 18. That's exactly the room I'm living in! I pick up the folder out of curiosity and run through the documents placed in it. Much to my amazement, it contains some half-torn papers on which songs are scribbled. I instantly recognize it as my mother's handwriting. This is unbelievable. While most of the papers have grown dark yellow and are no longer legible, I recognize a logo on one of the pages. It reads, 'Guardian Angel Home'. It's the same orphanage that Parvathi's mother works at. She has mentioned it to me quite a few times now.

I rush to Maria's room without saying a word to Akkriti. As I force open the door, I see Madhuri preparing her morning tea in one corner of the room. 'Wake her up. It's urgent,' I yell in excitement. Akkriti joins us thereafter.

'What's up with you? Is all good, girls?' Madhuri asks.

'Maria said the other day that I remind her of someone. Look here. This folder is full of my mother's documents. I accidentally found it in the attic.'

'This is very abrupt. You can't just enter and mess with things. She is old, she has Alzheimer's. She needs time to recall anything even if she has a connection to any of it, which I doubt.'

'I can't wait.'

'Which room number is mentioned on it?'

'18!'

'I have been working here for five years now. I know more than Maria knows. What is your mother's name?'

'Elisha.'

'Okay, I don't know any Elisha except for that famous singer who died long back.'

'She is my mother.'

'Are you guys taking drugs at Ricky's? That's one of the most stupid places here in Goa. I can see the impact on you. After performing there you have lost your sanity, Alara.'

'Madhuri, I can prove it, okay?'

'Just get out of here. Come back in the evening. I will speak with Maria, and also check the ledgers and the registers. Maria collects everything. She has this habit of not letting go of old crap. I know that because I have to keep cleaning and organizing her stuff,' she says in a frustrated tone. 'If there's any connection, we would definitely know.'

She drags us out of the room and shuts the door in my face. Akkriti tells me to be patient and fetches a glass of water for me.

'Are you really Elisha's daughter?' she asks, her eyes wide open in amazement.

'Yes, please keep it a secret. I don't want to fall under the local media's attention.' I suddenly realize that a lot of people know the truth now.

'You can count on me,' she smiles.

We walk back to the room. She tells me to go to the school with Ricky, and to also share the details with him. She assures me that Ricky would certainly be able to help me, much better than Madhuri.

I reach St. Paul's Hr Sec School just in time. Parvathi, Aarav, and Ricky greet me from a distance. While Ricky called me here and I invited Parvathi, I have no idea what Aarav is doing here.

'You're late,' Ricky snaps at me.

'Now he also knows?' I stare back at Ricky, pointing to Aarav.

'I am here to help.'

'Why?'

'That's what friends do. You helped me the other day. I rocked at my performance in Pune. Besides, I am a huge fan of Elisha. I would be the happiest person if I get to meet her once.'

I ignore most of what he says as I continue, 'Okay, I have something important to share before we start. Look here. I discovered this folder in Maria's store today. It has what supposedly are my mother's documents. What could it be doing there?'

Parvathi snatches the folder from me and opens it. She goes through the pages. 'Hey, this is the same orphanage where my mother works!'

'That's what!' I say.

'She was raised there. But she left it long back. There's hardly a chance that we will find something there,' Ricky comments.

'Ricky, we need to look at every place we possibly can. I set the rules of the game. That is how it works. Hope it makes sense to you all!'

'Calm down, we're together in this,' Aarav says, thereby easing the vibe.

We take a walk past the dead walls of the school that once existed. Never did Ricky mention that the school is not operational anymore. While I had a very different expectation of possibly meeting the Principal, new students, and old teachers, I find this place no short of an architectural heritage site begging for maintenance.

'Empires fall, glory fades, this remains standing tall in dull shades,' Ricky points to the walls as he continues, 'Someday, your material possessions are going to look like this. Gather experiences instead. Treasure memories. Spread love. Embrace life.' He laughs and gives gyan in his usual tone. But I feel mad at him. How could he be so cold-hearted towards his childhood friend?

'It feels like this whole thing is no more than a joke for him,' I tell Aarav as I feel helpless about being here.

I should rather have spent some time with Maria and tried to find out a lot more than I possibly can here.

'You may choose to enjoy the journey in this moment, or wait to arrive at the destination all the way. The choice is yours,' Aarav replies.

'The whole thing is about reaching the destination. I am not going back without my mom, or an answer perhaps!'

'That's not the point. Try to imagine your mother being here. Spending her childhood in those trees, sometimes hiding in the corridors.'

'I have imagined things for a long time now. I need results.'

'It is not going to be easy, you will need a release at some point in your life. The choice between tears and sweat will make all the difference. Don't be a crybaby.'

'Why do we need a teacher in life?' Ricky asks all of us, but I assume Aarav specifically.

'To be humble,' Aarav volunteers.

'What would Elisha answer? Do you guys know? I will tell you. She would say, to have some people in life one can make fun of. Don't judge her. We were in high school. She literally scared an entire class with a serial killer mask. She never got caught. You all know her as the dark and intense singer she was. But she wasn't that always. When I look back at our childhood, I remember her as a serious trouble maker.'

I smile. Then I smile wider. I break into laughter. I see the point. Ricky isn't so bad after all. He just wants to narrate his story right at the place where it happened.

'With our weekend performances, Elisha and I would make just enough pocket money to be able to afford our basic college expenses. I would buy some cigar like the British tourists for my teenage fixation to look cool and she would buy some new dresses for her next performance. She was so stylish and charming that people would fall for her even before listening to her melodious voice. And once they'd been held captive by her voice they would often return the next weekend with a couple more people. She was equally loved among the locals and the tourists.'

Parvathi interrupts, 'Why don't you play the drums anymore?' Ricky doesn't bother to answer, he rather takes a sip from his alcohol bottle. I don't really know the reason so I choose not to prod him any further.

'As she was raised in an orphanage, she longed for attention, longed for a loved one. Why do we want to feel protected? How will we grow? I used to tell her. But the worst thing she did was to leave her career and marry that stupid Czech NRI.'

'Mind your language. You're talking about my dad.' While I have a lot to settle with him myself, I certainly can't let Ricky abuse him for no reason at all.

'Okay, sorry!' he replies in a rude way.

'Tell me more.'

'About what?'

'Mom.' I demand, feeling weirdly like a stubborn young kid.

'I don't remember much. It has been a very long time now,' he says as he continues to walk ahead of us.

'Anything?'

'She loved dogs. Is that information?' He passes a wicked grin.

'Ricky, you really act weird at times. I thought we had something concrete to find here.'

'That's all I know, dear.'

'Aarav? Parvathi? Let's go back to the PG and try to find out more? Madhuri and Maria have a lot more information, I guess.'

Ricky grabs me by the shoulders and looks straight into my eyes. 'Everyone we know will leave us someday, Alara. You need to come to terms with the reality. I wanted to help you discover your mother's past so you could momentarily step into her shoes. If she were alive, she would have come back. Or at least written to me. I was her only family. If she didn't, she is not here in Goa.'

'What about the folder that I discovered in the morning?'

'She is famous now, isn't she? It could be some journalist who picked it up from the orphanage and forgot to return it for a long time. So many people now want to write on her, about her. The orphanage and the PG are hardly 2 km apart. Goa isn't that huge.'

'She is alive.'

'And nobody noticed? She is popular. Don't tell me it is to do with the plastic surgery shit from daily soaps.' These words by him make me hit rock bottom.

'Ricky, you're stubborn and selfish. Now I know exactly why she would not have come back to you,' I say and start walking back towards the PG. Aarav stays back with his foolish uncle, while Parvathi accompanies me.

'I will talk to mom and set up your visit soon. Maybe we can find something there.'

'Thank you, Parvathi. You are the only one that I can trust from the lot. Thank you for walking beside me.'

As I reach back, some people from the neighbourhood are gathered on the porch. They are standing in a circular formation. God knows if aliens have hit the land in between. I see Akkriti standing in the outermost circle. I walk up to her, 'What happened?'

'Lucky died.'

'What? How?'

'He did not wake up from his sleep.'

'He was Maria's life. She must be so upset. It's been a terrible day.'

I walk up to Maria as I say, 'He was a good soul.'

She looks at me with an undeterred face. She is composed. It feels as if she has come to terms with the fact that he had died long back.

'The weak try to control others. The strong are in control of themselves. Maria looks like a really strong person to me,' I tell Akkriti.

'The pain of parting with anyone is immense. But life is more about how you look at it than how it really is!' she smiles. 'I lost my family at the age of 5. I have been sold for trade multiple times. I still feel the pain but I can do nothing about it. Life is like that arrogant DJ who wouldn't take requests but play his own music. All you can do is wait till he plays your song and enjoy it while it lasts.'

She has a point. We keep quiet for a while. In the past few days, I started to love Lucky too. It just does not go down well with me. First, the fight with Ricky. Now, this. I can't even bother Maria about the documents today.

I walk back to my room. 'How have you been?' I hear Aarav with a gentle knock at my door. I don't know what to say as I don't know what would he be more interested in, knowing the truth or having a story that sells. There is this one thing about people and the whole world in general. Seldom does anybody want to know or appreciate the truth. Most of the time, they want to know a story that sells, catches eyeballs and can be spread like a rumour.

'How did you sneak in here? It's an all-women PG.'

'That's none of your concern. I wanted to share something important.'

'What's that?'

'To heal, you need to accept the truth,' he tells me as he moves away from where I sit. 'Uncle Ricky won't be lying. I have known him for quite some time. I agree he is a bit rude at times, but he has aged. Haven't you dealt with a grandparent before? '

'No, never.'

'See, as far as I know, he was in love with your mother. I guess he still is. He wants to believe that she is still alive, but he has come to terms with the fact that she died long back. And all that he said in the morning makes total sense to me.'

I sob as I look out of the window. The birds are chirping. The sun is about to set, and it's evening already. 'Accept?'

'You need to look at and accept the reality,' he says yet again as he puts a full stop to my apprehension.

'I feel empty. Lost. Vulnerable.' These are the exact words that come to my mind.

I keep staring out of the window as tears roll down my cheeks. I do not react, or move or respond to any of his questions. To me it's no more than background noise. I have always been the sunset kind of person. It was hard for me to imagine how some people woke up so energetic in the mornings, like Ricky. I can spend evening after evening at the park looking at the hues of the sky, birds chirping, returning home to their little ones. At least the birds returned to their little ones. They were not selfish like my mother. She never bothered to return.

The distant sound of the peeling of church bells often calms one's soul. I haven't known what calm means. For dictionaries can only create a recall, but experiences leave impressions on our soul.

I pick up a diary and a pen. 'I can't write,' I say and lose hold of my breath. 'I can't write a single word!'

'Relax!'

'What the fuck am I going to do then? This is how I earned my livelihood. What the fuck do I do if I cannot write new songs.'

'What happens when you start to write?' he asks politely. His face is as calm as the ocean today. Low tide it must be. When the ocean pulls the water back, it feels calm and silent.

'I know that you feel broken. But love is the only thing that can heal whatever is broken—the dreams or the heart. I kept running away from people who loved me but eventually found comfort only on returning.'

'What's the kind of love that heals? I'm sure I have not experienced it.'

'Or wait. Have you? If you've helped a specially-abled person cross the road and his/her smile seemed to make your day, yes you have! If you've cuddled with your dog after leaving him deserted for days, oh yes, you have! The kind of love that heals is selfless. Unfortunately, the kind of love that prevails is selfish. This is what Uncle Ricky does all the time. Add value to the lives of others around him.'

I hear Madhuri knock on the door. It scares the shit out of me. 'Hide,' I whisper aloud to Aarav.

'Where?'

'Under the bed. Right now!'

He follows my command. I swing open the door.

'I have checked the ledgers. A woman named Elisabeth occupied this room for six months, from December 1997 to July 1998. That's the closest name I could find to Elisha. I asked Maria but she does not remember a thing! I'm not sure if she's your mother because we don't have a last name. But here's the thing. Her occupation is mentioned here as nurse. I hope this helps.'

'Thanks!'

She leaves silently.

'Hey! Did you hear her?' I ask Aarav.

'Yes, I did!'

'My mother disappeared in Nov 1997. Can it be possible that she came all the way to Goa?'

'Without a legit passport? Visa? How is it possible? If she would have travelled with one, your dad and the police must have definitely known.'

155

'Under a false name or identity maybe? Elisabeth could be a false name?'

'We must visit the orphanage as well. Parvathi can guide us.'

'Yes, makes sense.'

'Will you promise me something, Alara?'

'Yes?'

'We would give it our best try. We may or may not find her. But you'll accept the reality that we discover, whatever it may be.'

'It's hard to commit. But I will give it my best effort.'

'Be ready at 11 AM tomorrow.'

'Why?'

'I am taking you to your mother's secret hideaway.'

'How do you know about it?'

'Ricky mentioned it to me.'

'I will ask Parvathi to join us. We can fix up a day visit to the orphanage.'

'Okay!'

'See you tomorrow.'

After Aarav leaves, the only thing I want to do is to call up my dad and ask him if he has any idea whether mom left Czech. But calling him will only interrupt my search, I fear, in case he has something to do with her disappearance. I keep tossing and turning in bed. I take a break and write a song for my next performance. After much effort spent in trying to sleep, I head to the shower.

Dreams hurt. Fears thwart. Obsessions take control.

But love, the kind that Aarav was talking about, nurtures. When the love is sexual, there's a relationship, with a defined beginning and end. For the desire eventually fades away, if not disappears completely. But in love devoid of all expectations, every day is a new beginning. Every fall is a new spring! This love isn't a destination; it's more like a journey. It's beyond bodies, yours and mine. It's the light of the soul. Lying naked next to someone, I could have felt incomplete. But as I sit naked beneath this flowing shower—hurt, vulnerable, and all by myself—I feel full of light and love. I strangely feel complete.

OUR SECRET HIDEAWAY—II

Aarav

Sunday, 8 December 2019
Canacona Island
Goa, India

'Love is the only thing that can heal whatever is broken—the dreams or the heart.'

I have moved to Goa for December. My semester exams are around the corner and so are the preparations for New Year's Eve in Goa. But I am more excited about being with Alara and preparing for my performance on New Year's Eve.

Although the unseasonal rains have turned monotonous, they feel special on this day. I am lying down in my bed and have passed five hours tossing from one corner to the other. I have pampered myself with dozens of cups of coffee and music.

At my hometown, Indore, it is quite different. Whenever it would rain, my mom would fry onion *pakoda*s for me and serve it with hot ginger tea. I have rejoiced most rains in my life with these utilities. But I have mostly been away these last six months. I am alone. I have not made new friends, except Alara. I stay in touch with the old ones though, but only telephonically. The memories with Tara have not yet faded away. Whenever the wind gets cooler and the weather gets windier, the clouds get darker more within than without.

But they say that having memories is like coming home to something! Surprisingly, they never mention whether they're good or bad memories.

I want to travel the whole world, perform in many more places, yet I don't wish to be known! It is crazy as to why someone would want to live a life where nobody really knows them. After all, after so much fame, money would follow, and isn't that what each one of us wants in life?

It is getting dark outside. It has been raining constantly since morning. But now it has got abrupt. It has taken its ferocious side and has bewildered people with thunder. The lightening got intense and could be heard as if every nanosecond. The mercury has also fallen by 10 degrees now. I feel cold as I move towards the window to bolt the shutters. I have moved into one of the huts at Ricky's.

It is small but exceptionally equipped to accommodate me. I repress my urge to shut the window, and instead sit beside it to enjoy the wonderful rains. As I wait for the clock to strike 11, it comes as a shock to me how unbearably slow each moment passes.

It's a quick boat ride that Alara and I would be taking to the nearby Canacona Island. I wish to share the bliss of this rainfall with her. As the roads are packed and the frogs are back, everything seems to say it out loud that it's a new season, a new beginning. Maybe it isn't too early, or too late, but the right time to express my desires to her.

I won't ask for much, just a glass of wine in the evening and a cup of coffee the next morning. Maybe that's not it, I want more, I want all of it. I find myself in a dilemma as it is hard to express into words, but the longing in my heart is simple proof that I also wish to be part of the time in between—the wine and the coffee.

You're not the perfect girl, the kind that books and movies talk about. You're not even close to my mother's definition of perfect. You're imperfect by all conventional definitions, yet I am deeply in love with you.

While I am lost in a world of my own making, Alara reaches Ricky's. Her presence feels as comforting as the taste of tea-dipped biscuits. Uncle Ricky and Alara share a cold stare. I guess I will have to make a lot of effort to patch things up between them.

Alara tells me, 'I feel that Maria is hiding something.'

'Why do you feel so?'

'I just don't know.'

'Okay, let's leave before it starts to rain again.'

'How are we going?'

'By boat.'

'What? Are you kidding?'

'No. I am very serious. Where is Parvathi?'

'They're busy with some new enrolments at the orphanage. She suggested that we tour the orphanage next week.'

'Oh!' I let out a sigh, but am inwardly too happy to have Alara by my side for the whole day.

I call up the local fisherman Deep who wears a cap like Captain America, and had promised me a ride in exchange for 500 bucks.

Twenty minutes later, we find ourselves right there, in the moment, cut off from all the worldly chaos. All we can hear is Deep rowing the boat, telling us weird stories every fifteen minutes or so of travellers he has met so far, and taking pride in his knowledge of the ocean vegetation, spotting dolphins, and fishing mackerels and pomfrets. He tells us how the hippies discovered Palolem and made way for Israeli travellers, Russians, and Europeans later on. After a few minutes, we reach a point where he has no more stories to share and he keeps rowing silently.

I close my eyes and start registering all the details in my head, like a true stand-up comedian. I keep having such conversations to bring real stories to life on stage, sometimes I overhear conversations in cafes too. A cold breeze flows from the other side of the ocean.

I soak in Alara's beauty along with the dolphins, aquatic vegetation, the crystal emerald coloured water, and above all the Goans, who are so pure at heart.

The beauty that I take in now reflects in my eyes. The next time any one of you meets me, you will see that in my eyes—the gates to my heart; and I would be absolutely delighted to share it through conversations about Goa. Believe me, you'll find the beauty in your eyes too. All I would ask you is—share this with anyone you meet, so the beauty of Goa lives on in our hearts forever.

He stops near the shore of the Canacona Island. This place looks like a landmass that has cut itself apart from the rest of the Palolem Beach. It might have been a part of it for a very long time but has turned out to be a different place altogether over due course of time. The waves continually make the rocks on its side slide back into the ocean. Uncle Ricky often mentions this place to me. Today, I want Alara to see the place her mother loved so much. I expect she will love it too.

'The beauty of this place is one of its kind.' I break the long silence between us.

'Irreplaceable. I can understand why mom loved it so much.'

'You know, the first step to every journey is to find oneself.'

'Yes, absolutely. I am happy to see you following your passion finally!'

'Alara,' I scream as I pace towards the inviting ocean, right behind her. It has been just a few days since I have known her, but everything about her, including her voice, is etched on my brain permanently. I had not expected her to come all the way to this place with me.

Is it something more than just following her mom's trail that has brought her here? The only way to find out is to ask her, but I can't gather the courage as of now.

She turns towards the direction of my voice. 'Is everything okay?' she inquires.

'The waves are very strong here. Don't enter the water if you can't swim?'

'Can you?'

'No.'

'But I can, so don't worry,' she laughs.

I watch her play on the beach. I take my diary out and start writing for the New Year's Eve performance.

'You are a coward!' she says as I shoot down her every effort to drag me into the sea. I give her all my attention, not missing even an opportunity to flirt with her.

'I will catch you!' she screams as she runs after me.

'Alara! You won't be able to,' I reply as I run away.

'I will,' she affirms and continues to chase me.

'As you wish,' I reply panting, as I stop a few meters away. She pants and walks slowly towards me.

I don't move an inch after this. We sit on the sand that glows against the sunlight. It starts to get colder. The adrenaline from the chase starts to fade away slowly. I feel a momentary chill wash down my body.

I rub my palms against each other to generate some feeble heat from the friction.

She does nothing but look at me, and for the first time since we met, I feel some depth in her action. She wears a blue shirt, blue as the deepest ocean, along with black shorts, both dripping with sea water.

I feel a bit awkward and gaze towards the sea. When you are attracted to someone, you tend to check them out, starting from places that you are most attracted to. I don't want to come across as a guy who ogles and stares. I need to win her over.

At that very instant I want to hold her, but my mind gets overwhelmed with thoughts. Maybe she has decided to play the chase because she is interested in me? Or maybe she just wants to make it easy for me to catch her? Or maybe she isn't fit enough to run some more? Men can never read women. It almost frustrates me.

Finally, I push myself back on the sand and lie there as I look towards the endless sky. She does the same. She continues to look at me. It's getting me equally excited and nervous. I stay calm.

'Alara! Isn't it beautiful to look at the sky, more alluring than portrayed in movies, even better than the books. Just hear the waves crashing against the shore at intervals and the silence in between. I feel spellbound.'

'Mhmm.' She continues to look at me instead.

'Believe me, Alara. Just do it.' She reluctantly looks at the sky.

'Why did you trust being with me on a secluded island?'

'I am grown up enough to take care of myself.'

'Okay! I am sorry. But will you tell me your intent of being at an unknown place?'

'I wanted to be with you. It's comforting, like a summer vacation,' she laughs.

'Are not you scared?'

'Scared of what?'

'Being all on your own, at a remote location, with no one around.'

'I am not alone, I would say. There's you!'

'What is your next song about?'

'It's about a girl being vexed by an intruder on a strange island,' she laughs out loud.

'You look beautiful when you laugh your heart out, and you look beautiful otherwise.'

'This is not going to work with me. Get better lines when you try to impress a girl next. Those imported from Bollywood are now hackneyed!'

'I was not trying to impress you. I was not flattering you either. I just said what I felt,' I say cheekily.

'I count on you.'

'Will you tell me something truly?'

'Oh yes! I certainly will, provided that you ask me truly.'

'What do you keep thinking about all day long? I find that most times you are lost in your thoughts. I may or may not be the only one to notice this. But the point is, don't you run out of thoughts while thinking so much?' I giggle as I speak.

'I think about life. I think about how complex it is. I am inquisitive. I seek answers to anything that causes doubt. I believe in asking questions rather than simply following the established constitutions. I am not a rebel, certainly not. But I am a wanderer. I keep flowing with the line of thought, questions, and ideas. There is no end to it. And so often I end up being lost in my own space. It may seem paradoxical, but I enjoy the moment by being in it, in my own world!'

'And I enjoy listening to you. I enjoy knowing you more. I enjoy sharing this space with you on the beach. I enjoy being with you, without a beer can. I enjoy watching you get lost in your own world. I enjoy seeing through your eyes. I enjoy the waves from the ocean touch our feet as we lie beneath the canopy of coconut trees. I enjoy the breeze playing with every inch of you. I also love the goose bumps on your hands at this very moment. So, is it the breeze or my words that are causing them?' I ask as I look straight into her eyes.

'The breeze!' she says confidently, looking right back into my eyes.

'Your eyes look more truthful.'

'You don't believe my words.'

'I don't!'

'I can make you faint with ecstasy without touching you.'

'Your voice does that to me all the time. I still remember when you performed at Ricky's for the first time. I have been listening to you on *YouTube* as well.'

'You've stalked me.'

'You're fairly popular!'

'You've mentioned Tara a couple of times. Do you mind sharing the story?'

'One of the nights this summer, I booked a cab and reached our apartment. We had been living in for 3 years by then. We went to the same university, fell in love, and decided to move in. She was fast asleep in the bedroom. I thought not to wake her up. I read a few messages on her phone and realized that she had started seeing someone else. Later, she told me that I misunderstood and it was some other shit. Finally, on my first visit to Ricky's, where she was supposed to join me, she messaged that she is getting married to a guy her family had scavenged for her. After she left, I worked on myself and discovered my love for comedy. It happened for the good. Let bygones be bygones.'

'Why did she have to remind you of your passion? What held you back earlier?'

'I am the youngest kid in the family. My parents decided to have me ten years after my elder sister. My father is going to retire before I complete college. I just have some responsibilities and so the internship at the bank is something I continue to keep.'

'Do you still love her?'

'I loved her until I met you.' My feet go cold and my head goes numb. I am not ready for another rejection yet. But I let out the truth in the nick of time.

She moves her face closer to mine and closes her eyes. This moment is something I have been waiting for days now. I move forward and kiss her. A perfect kiss seldom happens under the perfect circumstances. A perfect kiss is unplanned, extremely passionate.

As I lie next to her, I ponder upon every inch of her body. She does not look perfect. I discover. There are scars on her back. But it's utterly crazy how none of it matters to me. I still want to kiss her—especially the scars, each one of them, one by one. There is something so intense I feel for those scars. I can almost feel the pain that she must have gone through when she got them in the first place. I want to whisper it into her ears, 'None of it matters to me.'

And I know that they're not the only scars. There are some that she hides behind that smile. I know they did hurt her at a point in her life, and some of them continue to haunt her. I whisper into her ears, 'None of it matters to me.'

This is what love does to you. It makes you look beyond what you see. Above all, it makes you look beyond what others can see!

As she directs me while we make love, her voice isn't soothing, but often commanding and strong. Unlike her, I sing awfully. But the conversations that we have, you and I, stay in my head, beautiful like the images ingrained on stones of a heritage building. Your words are like pieces of art that cling to the walls of my heart. And yes, I want you to talk to me all this time.

Her anger isn't perfect. It makes her look like a wicked monster as she shouts and makes me feel miserable. Her tongue isn't perfect and craves for everything mine doesn't. I don't like to eat salads as she does. I prefer pizzas all the time.

All I want from her is to part her lips again to kiss me hard. I am imperfect by every measure, yet it is in her arms that I feel perfect by any measure. And all this time she makes me feel imperfect by making me do things that I had only dreamt about so far.

I love to play with her legs, and I love it even more when occasionally her legs play with mine against the sand. She touches me in places no one was allowed to and no one has yet, but it feels like prayer.

When we regain our senses, I realize that this moment between us might not last forever, that the sun would be up to lighten the vistas drenched in rains, that this moment was ephemeral. But I wouldn't be able to thank the universe enough for this ephemeral moment when I could feel 'forever'.

Love is the only thing that can heal whatever is broken—the dreams or the heart. Making love to someone is like having the key to unlock their deepest secrets. The conversation that follows flows effortlessly. It's like breaking the barrier of ego in front of at least one person and becoming the real you for a while. The need to lie fades as much as the need to please someone. You become just you, as you are, beautiful inside out.

'What's the craziest thing you guys do in college?' she asks as she dresses up and throws my clothes on my face.

'We make every guy dress up like a girl and dance like a stripper on their birthday. In fact, last week, a batchmate of mine accidentally played an adult film on the projector during the final viva. Is it any different in Prague?'

'I should have attended college in India. It's fun back there, but it sounds a lot more fun here.'

'What do you like about me?'

'You mostly smell like cigarettes and black coffee. And when it rains, I want to have you right next to me, to make me feel light-headed like cigarettes do and to provide me with the warmth of black coffee. I am drawn to men who smoke, I find them irresistible. You aren't all things great but all things imperfect, and it is this imperfection that drives me crazy!'

'That's poetic.'

'What do you think of the sea?'

'If I had to describe the sea in three words, they would be—endless, eternal, thought provoking.'

'What thought does it provoke in you, at this very moment?'

'There is always a sunrise somewhere. While the sun is setting here for us, it's rising in some other part of the world. It is all one's perspective.'

'And death? Does it mean a new life?'

'Death is a mystery, Alara. But they say death does make way for new life. Every part of our body will become a part of the universe again. The only thing that is life is the continuity, the soul.'

'Indeed.'

I walk towards my side and set a heap of twigs and branches on fire. Thankfully, it isn't raining and Captain America has left the woods.

'Have you ever stared at the stars? Or at the fire? It's the same, isn't it? Stars are burning gases in the galaxy too. But since the stars are far away, their heat doesn't hurt you as much as the fire near you. Time can change perspective and heal everything. In the darkest of the dark, there is light.'

'That's thoughtful!' says Alara.

'What's on your mind?'

'Mom. As always.'

'We'll find her, together, I promise!'

'I trust the one I love but I can never trust love itself.'

'Nothing is more important than your smile, laughter. Rest can be taken care of!'

'What do you think is the most important thing while being in love?'

'Uncle Ricky often mentions that respecting the other person's individuality when in love is very important. I kind of agree with most of the things he says.'

She instantly hits me on my back. Women hit men everywhere, in restaurants, cafes, bars, when they are happy and when they are sad.

'He is a good fellow. You need to patch up with him.'

'Life isn't beautiful! Yes, that's how it is. But somehow, love empowers life to feel beautiful. My love for you does that to me. Although I have met you now, I feel as if I have always known you. You are exactly the one I wished for, one with whom I would travel to countries far off, one to hold my hand as I sip the morning coffee in my hotel balcony, to wander aimlessly on the streets, to get lost in animated conversations, holding a glass of wine! Now that I have found you and there's no time machine, let's go back to those places and live out all of my fantasies.'

'How did you like the place?'

'It's the best kept secret, yours and mine.'

Life is imperfect and all you can do is seek happiness in the imperfections. You're my adventure and I seek all the thrill in your imperfections. I crave for those perfect moments placed beautifully between the imperfect. I long for another today soon!

THANK GOD IT'S SATURDAY

Ricky

Saturday, 21 December 2019
Ricky's Beach Shack
Palolem, Goa, India

'When your heart breaks, every passing day, it
opens you up to new possibilities, often helping
you emerge as the best version of you.'

Sheen has this habit of chalking out the thought of the day on the black board placed in front of Ricky's. She finds bliss in reliving her school days with this gesture every day. Today, it reads:

Bad News:
No matter how hard you try to protect yourself, one day, your heart will break.

Good News:
When your heart breaks, every passing day, it opens you up to new possibilities, often helping you emerge as the best version of you.

Romeo reads the board out loud and drags a chair to our table. 'Would you mind if . . .'

I cut him short, 'Sit, bro.' Sheen instantly smiles and walks towards the kitchen to order another coffee. That's the thing about Ricky's. We have so many repeat customers and friends that time passes by and we don't even realize where it went!

'You were supposed to visit last night,' I break the silence.

'Oh! One of Shankar's clients slipped in the Mandovi River.'

'What was he doing?'

'Taking a selfie!'

'Tourists are a nuisance. They do awful things and bring a bad name to Goa.' He looks disturbed but I can't stop myself from cursing. I have no empathy for young kids abusing smartphones.

'We're expecting a lot more tourists this December,' he says.

'Good for our shack's business. All the rooms are already sold out for New Year's Eve.'

'Have you aligned your artists yet? The ones who will perform on New Year's Eve?'

'For the stand-up act I am sure of Aarav. Still looking for singers. Most of the artists are booked for the Goa Music Festival.'

'How about Alara?'

'She is upset with me. She won't perform.'

'That's bad! Good luck hunting!'

'If you could go anywhere in the world and do anything you wanted, what would it be?' I had asked Romeo this when he visited my place for the first time.

'A taxi driver on an isolated island by choice, as there would be no one from his family to judge him,' Romeo had suggested.

Now, Romeo runs his own taxi agency. He earns a commission for all the ad-hoc tourists he gets for us. He also helps us with the airport/railway station pick-ups/drops for our guests. Romeo worked as a chartered account in Mumbai before he took an early retirement.

That's the thing about Goa. It does not let you stay away for long. Sooner or later, it calls you back. Romeo is one of the very first guys I helped realize their dreams.

Let me ask you this, what would you be if you were stranded on an island?

At least pick a Saturday now and then and make it your private island. Be whoever you want to be, do whatever the day wants you to do. Aarav, I am excited to watch you perform tonight.

A lot of people have gathered tonight to watch Aarav perform and I am sure that he will rock the audience for sure. Sheen and I gesture at him with our thumbs up.

He moves to the stage, clears his throat, and greets everyone with a wide smile. He exudes the exact amount of confidence that I have been hoping from him since the first time we met. He pulls in a huge amount of air as he shoots:

Okay, is it misogynistic if I have a hotness scale? This is in my mind. It is constantly rating people around me.

Is it wrong? Hmm . . .

The audience, mostly the women in it, go 'booo'. Some of the men start hooting.

Okay okay, I see what's happening here. I know men are assholes, but we came calibrated with this shit.

All of you women, look around you. It's not just me, all the guys have it and do it all the time.

So let me raise an olive branch here. I don't have it only for women. I do it to guys too.

I have a hotness scale for guys too. Am I still misogynistic?

Some woman in the crowd asks, 'What's the scale?'

Hahaha. So it's a basic scale of 1 to 10.

10 has Chris Hemsworth. That chiselled body. But only as Thor. Otherwise he is a 9. Same with Ryan Reynolds. He is 10 as himself but 11 as Deadpool.

Cause Deadpool rules.

9 are superstars, footballers, and such.

8 are other actors like SRK and Tom Cruise.

7 are sub-standard stars and place holder.

5 is me, between dumb guy in chemistry and Zakir.

No body gives a fuck about the 2s and 3s. These are the Rameshs and the Jerrys in your life.

1 are special people. One are like . . . not Jerrys. They are different. One are like . . .

Like 1 is MJ. The Michael Jackson. I know! Great music, but child molester. Great music though. Thriller was a bomb. But do you want to be that person who fucks Michael fucking Jackson and then steals his nose.

Hahaha. It's like, that man is made of papier mâché. I really believe there is an MJ sex tape somewhere, but instead of a sex tape it turned into a jigsaw puzzle after one passionate thrust.

He enacts what he says. The entire club is filled with laughter, noise, and chatter. This has been Aarav's best performance so far! I make my way through the over-enthusiastic crowd by slightly pushing each one that comes in my way.

'I am sorry about the other day, but I always knew you would perform this well one day!' I say to him.

'I owe my life to you, Uncle Ricky. Thank you,' he laughs and cries at the same time.

'When you make your own path, it is not an easy journey. You will most likely suffer. You will fail many times. But trust me, there will also be moments when you will shed tears of sheer happiness. And that's not only an extraordinary feeling but a rare one too.'

'This is just the beginning!'

'By the way, is Alara still upset with me?'

'Of course, she is! We must make an attempt to make things better.'

'I think she must perform at the New Year's.'

'She must, but I guess she won't be performing until she finds Elisha. She needs closure.'

'Everyone needs closure. Even I need one. But after so many years of her disappearance I have come to accept the fact that she has most possibly died. I want to believe very much that Alara finds her, but it seems almost unbearable to carry this hope buried within me.'

Let me read this out to you from my diary. With the events that have unfolded in the last few days, I have started penning a lot of my feelings down:

Dear My Past Self,
I wish you knew that you will finally make it. I wish
I could tell you not to cry on sleepless nights. I wish
I could tell you that you deserve every dream that
you wish to achieve.

'What is love according to you?' Aarav asks.

'Love defies rules, knows no limits, and chooses to be ever-giving.'

'What is passion according to you?'

'Passion sets our hearts on fire and frees us like a mighty eagle.'

'What if she decides to never come back to perform here?'

'No matter how hard you try, some relationships will never go back to the way they were. Acceptance is peace. If she chooses not to, I'm okay with that.'

I roam around the world to search of you but come back home to feel you within. We all take different journeys to reach the same destination—being at peace with ourselves. Some meditate, some pray, I often dive and surf as the ocean keeps calling me in my dreams and reality alike.

'How was your Dad's retirement party that happened last week?'

'It was an amazing night filled with a mix of emotions. It was so wonderful to hear him speak to a larger audience, and while everyone spoke about retirement as *the end*, he spoke about it as *the beginning*.'

'The beginning?'

'Yes! I'm sure he'll follow his passion and come up with some breakthrough research in mathematics soon.'

He takes his smartphone out to show me the pictures from the party. I don't really allow smartphones near me, but I forgive him this time.

'This picture of us is the best one I have and it speaks volumes about how much mom and dad have taken care of me. Also, I feel that all the sarcastic humour I have is my father's legacy!'

'Although your dad and mom are alien to the concept of stand-up comedy as they have been government employees, I will make sure they never impose their choices on you. I will always encourage you to work towards your dream.'

'That's why I say, I owe my life to you.'

'What else?'

'There's no greater joy than falling back on those who will always be there for you. Maybe that's the reason why despite being miles apart your heart belongs to your loved ones, your home. It felt amazing going back home. Since my breakup with Tara, I have been avoiding it for a very long time. But when your mother cooks your favourite dish, your father makes sure that your house looks perfect, your sibling snatches away savouries from your hand, you realize that nothing has really changed in all these years that you have been away from home, only that the bond has grown stronger with every passing year.'

'I wish I never know of familial bonds. I find a home in the bond I share with nature.'

'Why did you never marry?'

'Aarav, I really loved Elisha. I still do. I never felt the same way for any other woman. I have been dating women casually, but never did it ever occur to me that I could marry them while I was with them.'

'I think Sheen loves you. You must give it a shot.'

'I am supposed to drag you out of your break-up. Not the other way round. Mind your own business, son.'

I laugh out loud.

'Why did you stop playing the drums? Who was the guitarist?'

'Will tell you some other day. Not in the mood today.'

'If we find Elisha, will you play the drums again?'

'Maybe, yes!'

'I am glad that I now have three reasons to find Elisha!'

'Don't be too optimistic.'

'What could have happened to her?'

'I can't comment on that. I was away when all the news of her flooded the market. I really don't know. But what I know for sure is that she never returned.'

We keep chatting for hours until the sun arrives to announce the beginning of another day. Late night conversations with someone you bond with are one of the greatest assets in the treasure of your memories. I remember every such conversation I have had with Elisha.

I tell Aarav, 'The most successful people are not the most talented ones, but the stronger ones who keep at it and do everything to realize their dreams.' I then leave for my morning run and Aarav crashes into the bed of his coco-hut.

WITHOUT YOU, WITH YOU

Alara

Wednesday, 25 December 2019
Guardian Angel Home
Goa, India

'To have an infinite capacity to love is the greatest act of courage.'

If there is something I wish to do at all, it is to add to the others around me and never subtract anything from them. I rub my eyes as I welcome the Christmas morning sun. It is going to be special indeed. I'm finally visiting my mother's orphanage today. Parvathi is going to join us anytime.

'You must wear red today,' Akkriti says as she enters my room.

'Why?'

'It is Christmas. Shouldn't you be the Santa for the kids at the orphanage?'

'That's a good idea. I must pick up some chocolates on the way.'

'Is Aarav joining?' she asks in a teasing tone.

'Yes. He will come directly to the orphanage.'

'What are you more excited about?'

'You're overthinking!'

'Every person newly in love lives in a state of denial.'

'Love is a powerful word.' I combat every effort she makes at teasing me.

As I reach the orphanage I am guided to Principal Joseph's office. Neither Parvathi nor Aarav are anywhere to be seen. These guys are never on time. He greets me with a smile and suggests that I motivate the students for the upcoming exams. I agree to it without a second thought. As I walk through the orphanage with an assistant teacher, she tells me that this place has developed much beyond an orphanage now. It has a fully functional hospital and school too. We head towards the school.

I reach one of the classes and greet the students with a smile. I speak to them about my journey so far as a singer. I also tell them about Aarav. Much to my amazement, they are excited to know more and more.

I am amazed to see how well-informed they are—from Ed Sheeran to Elon Musk to A.P.J. Abdul Kalam to KFC stores, they are inspired by the journeys of artists, entrepreneurs, innovators, and leaders from all over the world.

We discuss the importance of having a purpose in life, a goal that keeps pulling us towards the destination, and enjoying the challenges presented by life as the journey progresses. I reassure them that their skills will help them touch the sky and it's irrelevant that they were abandoned. They have found the right community. I tell Elisha's story to inspire them beyond measure.

On repeated requests by the students, one of the kids called Vishal performs a rap song. I encourage them to follow their dreams and to keep at their inner calling despite the challenges they would face. I feel glad to have chosen to spend my day with them. I share with them that the most successful man is one who adds value to the ones around him and believes in nurturing the society as a whole.

'Before I leave, I have a question for you all. What is the one thing that sets you apart from others?'

While everyone gives it a try, I love this one the most: 'A smile on your face sets you apart from others. There are some feelings which will be there even after we are all long gone. Our bodies might become a topic of research, but our stories will be passed on from one generation to the other. The more love we share, the more we would help shape a loving world!'

And yes, amidst all the chaos, the bliss is in sharing a smile, a word, or a gesture of love. Go ahead. Make a person smile today. Anyone, anywhere! At your office, cafeteria, metro train, taxi—the choice is yours! When you come back home, your problems might still be the same, but you will have found the courage to sail through! Millennials, we are much more than blindfolded consumers; we are loving and caring human beings, and there's more to our lives than owning the latest gadgets! I am glad that even though these kids are not the chosen ones, they are choosing to live their dreams.

'Don't let anyone tell you that you're born ordinary. Not even your teachers. Nothing is determined at birth. Extraordinary results come from extraordinary efforts,' I tell them as I sign off from the session.

Aarav joins in. He is wearing a cobalt blue shirt. The inner lining of his collar is visible till it converges at the first button. I look at him with the concentration of a saint. I imagine myself wearing the same shirt and getting morning coffee for him.

I ask him, 'Where were you? Today is an important day!'

'Uncle Ricky and I kept chatting till late in the night. I missed the alarm and the subsequent snooze. I am sorry!'

'It's okay. Let us go to the office. Lakshmi might be here by now.'

As we head back to the office, Lakshmi and Parvathi are already there, waiting for us.

Parvathi asks with excitement, 'How did the session go? I'm hopeful that you must have enjoyed interacting with the kids here.'

'These kids are bright indeed. They have a lot of potential. They will reach for the stars.'

'This is my mom, Lakshmi. She is really glad to meet you guys.'

'Hello, aunty. Happy to meet you as well.'

'Parvathi keeps telling me about you guys every day. Although I am meeting you for the first time it feels as if I have known you for a very long time,' she says as she walks closer to me. Her eyes fill up with tears and she gently pats my cheeks.

'That's true, we have become such good friends in such a short span of time. That is pretty unbelievable.'

'Is he also a good friend?'

'Yes, meet Aarav. He is another good friend I have made in Goa.'

'Alara, I have something with me that I have to share with you,' she says in a low tone and silently walks to an old cupboard that occupies one corner of the room. She takes out an envelope from which she skilfully extracts a piece of old paper, which has gone yellow and is torn at the sides. She hands it over to me.

'Would you mind if I asked you to excuse us for a while?' Lakshmi asks Aarav, indicating him to leave the room.

'Absolutely not. Alara, I am taking a walk around. See you.' He shuts the door close.

I start to read it aloud in my mind:

Dear Alara,
Have you ever seen a bird cage stuffed with Christmas lights used for decoration? If I have to sketch my soul on paper, give it a shape, that's exactly how it looks. My freedom has been curbed like a bird in a cage but my spirit shines endlessly like the lights. The beauty of light is that a miniscule

part of it will penetrate any wall. My soul is trapped but it will continue to shine and light a million other lives till I take my last breath, and even after. When a soul has a reason to live, no matter how many times it has been trapped, it eventually sets itself and a million others free.

Since getting married to your dad, I have been running from life. Sometimes for you, sometimes from him, sometimes with me. But I don't wish to run anymore. Specially, not from myself. Goa is my old home, my new life. I am happy here, just by myself. And every time it rains, I play my guitar. I play when it's sunny too. My passion is an inseparable part of me. Now, I'm not running after anything, I'm walking to the core of me.

Cheating on your loved one is easy. Stranding them and moving on with someone else, easier. But remember, life has its own ways to teach you! Today on the better side, someday you will be on the other side. I have been cheated and I tried my best to make the marriage work. But when I realized I can't do anything about it, I came back to India.

I was hoping to come back someday and get your custody when I become financially independent. On the other hand, counting today, I don't know if I even have ten more days until I take my last breath. I feel I have lost the courage to fight anymore.

But never hate your dad or me, we love you in our own ways. Remember, to have an infinite capacity to love is the greatest act of courage. You've been hurt. But who hasn't? Yet, choose to love everything, everyone around. It will make you the strongest of all.

The ones you love bring out the best in you but also hold the potential to bring out the worst in you. It's you who needs to build the right perspective to live a fulfilling life.

I want to return, I really do. But I don't know how long I will be able to fight.

If you've picked up singing from me, love, my last wish is that you complete my album and release it. There's a wooden box in the attic which contains some of my unfinished songs.

Will love you for eternity,
Elisha

'What could I have done?' I ask Lakshmi, helplessly. I thump my fists on the table. No one utters a single word.

'What could I have done?' I sob helplessly. I look at my own reflection in the window pane on the other end of the room. I have not felt so helpless before.

'Not every dream comes true. Sometimes, we need to find the courage to accept the reality and live with it,' Lakshmi says as she picks me up.

'Did she take her life?'

'She came back to find Ricky and started performing again, but Ricky had left by then. New performers had replaced them at the Hippie Trails Cafe. She started working as a nurse here.'

'Did she stay at Maria's PG? Madhuri told me the other day that a nurse occupied that place briefly for six months. Also, Maria mentioned that I remind her of someone.'

'Yes, she did live in the same room where you're staying.'

'You did not answer. Did she take her life?'

'She was struggling hard to make ends meet and had no support except for us. Also, her singing career had taken a backseat. Her relationship with your father turned worse after their divorce when she got to know that he was marrying again.'

'Does my dad know the truth?'

'Yes, he does. I called him up after the incident happened. He felt really sorry. Your dad and I decided to acknowledge Elsiha's last wish, to hide the truth from you. She had asked me to hand you this letter only if you chose to come find her someday. I never read the letter before she committed suicide so I never knew what the future held. Your dad sends huge funds to us every year. It's because of his support that we've been able to run so many vertices and bring out the best in the kids at the orphanage.

The hospital is named Elisabeth Nursing Home after you mother.'

'Was that her true name?'

'Elisha was her stage name. Sister Angela had named her Elisabeth as she loved reading Portuguese Literature. We found here at the park, abandoned at the age of one probably. We've buried her as Elisabeth in the park. The fact that her stage name and real name are different helped us maintain the secret of her disappearance.'

'Did Parvathi know?'

'Yes, she did. We wanted you to live like your mother for some days, feel her presence in the best way possible, before telling you the truth. It was our plan. We really want you to fulfil her last wish of releasing the album.'

'Who else knows?' I shout out loud.

'No one out of this room except for your Dad. Aarav and Ricky know as much as you know. Now that you know the truth, it's up to you whether you wish to tell others or not.'

'Did you tell my dad that I am here?'

'Not yet,' she murmurs. Parvathi watches the scene silently. What could she say anyway? She has been the friend I trusted, the friend who cheated me.

'I need some time with myself,' I pick up the letter and make a move towards my room. I don't bother Aarav. I just want to be with myself.

Her letter feels like darkness at the end of a tunnel. My decision to keep at my dreams and find you someday kept me happy on most days, mom. But today, I feel wounded. I feel deserted. I feel as if I have failed to find you.

I feel hurt, hurt really deep. But it's not like the wound you might get when you go for running and fall, nor the kind of hurt that slipping your hand off a knife would cause. It's the kind of hurt so deep that I believe I might as well die.

Oh! Did I forget to mention that I am contemplating death? Right now. Well, yes I am.

It is not because of the pain that this kind of hurt causes. It's for the pleasure that freeing myself of this burden would offer—the burden of never meeting you again. No, I'm not at fault. Don't blame me. Like I've told you, my soul tricked me into this. Yes, it did. The only wrong I did was listen to it. If I would not have come all this way to search for you, I would have died with the hope that you're alive somewhere.

But tonight, I am not going to listen to it. I have made up my mind. I would rather talk to it. I would want it to see the consequences of luring me to follow my dream. Eventually, I would either talk it out of this or die. But there's no way I'm carrying this burden any further.

But how do you know the kind of hurt I'm talking about? You can imagine it if you have ever experienced a dream shattering into a million pieces like glass. If you're one of those people who have been wary of the consequences of dreaming and, therefore, have not dreamt thus far, you're not courageous enough. Maybe even the wise aren't spared by the trap of love, and if not dreams, I'm sure love wouldn't have spared you from feeling this—the kind of hurt that I am talking about. The hurt of someone close to you leaving you forever, or passing away.

I enter my room and collapse into a pile of nothingness due to the dizziness that this kind of hurt causes. I want to tell you, my soul, that you did a terrible thing by fooling me into following my dream.

Often in the moments of extreme pleasure or pain, you tend to blur out the wider picture and focus on the immediate things around you. My hair fall over my face and I feel surrounded by darkness, except for the thin streams of light from the bulb in my room filtering through the locks of my hair.

I light a cigarette I had bought on the way back. I am not a smoker, but I need something to occupy my time with. And if it deteriorates my health, damages me, I am more than happy to spend time with it. What I can see and feel with utmost clarity are the strands of hair that smell like burnt cigarettes, cigarettes that we often light in the company of bleeding dreams or burning desires.

Why do we seek solace in hurting ourselves when we're at the lowest? At this very moment, I want to skin myself layer by layer and reach the place where my soul exists. For if the tree is uprooted and thrown away, there would not be the expectation of it bearing a fruit someday! For if the strings are pulled and plucked from the guitar, there would not be an expectation of it to sooth the ear someday!

I move to the bathroom and reach out for the blade in my razor. I want it to rip my skin, layer by layer precisely. As I am about to touch it to my wrist, the letter drops out of my pocket and falls on the ground near my feet. I look at it and I am instantly reminded of my mother's wish to release the album.

Selfless love is true love. It permeates the subtleties of the timeline, irrespective of the timeline's orientation—alternate reality or rebirth. That's the kind of love that poets have penned down for ages across geographies. It's eternity. It's forever. It's the kind of love that teaches you to give, not expect, and not only to give but to do so with a whole heart. Feeling such love can prove to be one of the most ennobling experiences of your life. No matter who you are, what you do, or where you go, this love will stay within you, for it is beyond the constraints of time and space. Like for me, my mother's love would. Forever.

I throw the blade away and sit on the floor. I crawl towards my side. My legs aren't hurt but I just don't feel like getting up, so I choose to crawl. I move out of the bathroom but keep lying on the floor, my eyes closed, my mind unable to think anymore.

After a few minutes, I feel that I should stop right away for I might cause damage that I'll repent for years. And if I die, I would cause damage that the world would repent for years.

'I won't do the same,' I scream as I catch hold of the loose strands of my hair and pull them back, forcefully placing them behind my ears.

I stand up and pull out the wooden box. That's all my mom, who perhaps loved me deeply, has left behind. I go through the songs, scribbled pages, everything.

In that very moment it strikes me that I have been gifted, gifted with the ingenious ability to translate these moments into songs and help a million others who may be contemplating 'death' in this moment, every moment. I could save a few, if not millions. I realize that I am sent to this world with a purpose and I am lucky enough to discover it at a young age.

But this isn't exactly the person within me who tells me this. It is actually my mom who left this letter behind. She loved me immensely and I can't let her down. Who knows if the whole theory that souls don't die is true? My soul is connected to hers as it is to a million others. We're all bound by the force of love. And this is how my soul chooses to convince me when I am at my lowest.

I eventually decide to surrender to it, listen to it, like I always do. It is said that the collective consciousness of humanity knows the future, directs the future, that it is all written, and that I would have to finish the album.

When I listen to the voice within me, I contemplate life. Not just tonight. Every time. I listen to the soul and choose not to talk any further. The worship is done. I feel as if I have regained all my energy, and I wipe my tears as I prepare myself for a new dawn.

Aarav knocks on the door. 'Alara, I love you. I promise to be with you through this! Tell me, what is the matter with you?'

'You've come here at the right time,' I say as I open the door and hug him.

'Why did you leave abruptly without informing me. Is all good? Parvathi told me that you left for Maria's.'

'I hope that someday you will realize how difficult it is to live with someone who you know is not here to stay.' I lose patience and say, 'My mother took her life. We will never find her.'

There is something so strange with this relationship. A step ahead and I might not be able to take the responsibility, a step back and I fear I will lose Aarav! 'I just want this to stay, the way it is right now,' I tell him.

'I am here!'

'I fear that as time progresses, I might lose you as I lost my mother.'

He fetches me a water bottle. I sit beside him. We don't talk to each other for almost an hour. I sit sobbing silently and he pats my back. Time passes by. Time stands still. Later, I narrate to him all that happened at the orphanage.

'Uncle Ricky would hate this news!' Aarav says.

'I think he is wise to have come to terms with reality long back. Unlike me.'

'He wanted the truth to be otherwise.'

'Would you perform with him for New Year's?'

'Would he ever play the drums?'

'I will convince him. Don't worry. Wherever Elisha is, she would love to see this collaboration!'

'I wish she is watching!'

Next morning, I go back to the orphanage and apologize to Parvathi and Lakshmi. They take me to my mother's gravestone. I offer her flowers and spend the day at the park finishing the songs for the album. I finally turn my phone on for a while and text dad, 'We may not approve of each other, dad, but we can definitely accept each other. I am staying in India until the end of February. I have found a home. Home is a state of mind. Home is togetherness. Or maybe, home is the people who love you. Or it's that feeling which doesn't let you leave a place. What I know for sure is that home isn't made of bricks and mortar. Nor is it the expensive sofa in your living room. It's not the lavish balcony onlooking the city, but the conversations with your people in that balcony which become memories forever. It is not an incomplete family picture that hangs in the living room. I can vouch for this as I have felt it so strongly within my heart, time and again, since the moment I landed in India.'

WHAT BREAKS YOU,
IT MAKES YOU

Aarav

Tuesday, 31 December 2019
Ricky's Beach Shack
Palolem
Goa, India

'Some dreams can never come true.
While some can.'

Ricky has been depressed ever since I told him the truth. Sheen and I have made numerous efforts at convincing him to play the drums again, but all have been in vain. It's New Year's tonight and I just wish that I succeed at my last attempt. I have asked Alara to reach Ricky's early in the morning at seven. Together, we will try to move the stubborn Ricky.

The board in front of Ricky's today reads:

It's New Year again! But did you really get a chance to reflect upon the last year? If yes, did you jot down your learnings?

Here is ours: Set fitness goals, sing your heart out loud, dance to the sound of the ocean, travel more, think beyond set limits, explore the inner you, dare to dream, and believe in LOVE.

I greet Ricky. He is busy attending to clients. Ricky's is done up in balloons of yellow colour. Alara pulls a chair next to me as she joins me. After making me wait for half an hour, he comes and joins us at the table.

'Nice write up on the board,' I tell Ricky.

'Sheen has put it up.'

'What are YOUR learnings?' I ask with curiosity.

'My biggest learnings are very similar to the kind of experiences I had on the ocean. Do what you love and do more of it. In my case, I love floating on the ocean and, therefore, make sure that I go back to the ocean when I need to heal. This process is like meditation for me. Circumstances are just like the waves of the ocean. The more you try to fight them, the more you struggle and eventually lose. Can you really challenge Mother Earth? But the more you loosen yourself, the farther you move. In fact, the waves then help you move. So, let loose of the circumstances, you can't really control things external to you.' He takes a short pause as he continues, 'Some dreams can never come true.'

'While some can,' Alara says as she interrupts Ricky. 'One such dream is my mother's last wish that I record an album. I feel it's incomplete without you playing the drums.'

Ricky doesn't speak for a while. There is an awkward silence.

'Why don't you say yes? I remember that we spoke about closure. Would this not be it?'

'I can never forgive myself. She came back but I had left. She had no family,' he sobs. I was seeing

Ricky shed tears for the first time. He was always my iron man otherwise.

'You can't go back and rewrite the past, but you can write the present and build a better future,' Alara interrupts.

'Alara, when will you let the truth out in public? I believe that her real story needs to be known. Media has reported really nasty stuff about her.'

'Not now! I have planned for the right moment, the right day already.'

'Okay!' Uncle Ricky says.

'Okay what?' I ask him teasingly.

'I will play the drums tonight.'

Alara looks at me as she smiles. Finally, we could do this. A crowd as huge as I had never seen before gathers at Ricky's at night. Every table, every room is booked. In fact, there's no space to even walk around where the stage is set.

The crowd can be seen scattered all the way down to the shoreline. Extra tables have been set up by the sea.

I walk up the stage, grab the mic, and say:

I don't know if I will make you laugh tonight, but I will surely tell you a story, my story. My old story and my new story.

So, sometimes life is about being the hero of your story. But not all of us are heroes. Why?

Why can't we just become heroes?

211

Due to the judgement passed on by the all-good all-righteous society. Trust me. I was constantly being judged for doing nothing too. So I told myself, fuck it. Fuck this shit. Now I live preaching the philosophy of Hakuna Matata, non-Disney translation: no fucks given.

Judging someone is like rating people for their choice of colour, I can't dislike someone because I don't like yellow.

We live in a country which is genetically predisposed to talk shit about others. We are not the fastest, or the smartest, we are not beautiful but when it comes to trash talk, we can make Gossip Girls cry.

A few things are like jerking off. Everyone does it, but no one wants to talk about it. But I will talk about me. Ricky says it's a story that needs to be told out loud.

I RECENTLY PUT MY PAPERS DOWN. Finally. I am jobless. The decision was tough but not as tough as the painstaking task of stacking filled bottles in the fridge during summers. I hate doing that. Really. If I had to make a list of chores I hate, it would be like: 1. My job, 2. Filling bottles, 3. Taking care of an infant. They are sticky, leaky, and germy. I rest my case.

Try and go back to your parents and tell them that you've quit your job today. That is the moment you'll know seeking support is like seeking a mirage. Only you can support yourself, you do not need anyone.

Job is not the problem. Our mentality is flawed in the first place. We get an MBA to seek jobs. Why don't we think of setting our own business? I am happy that my colleague Shikhar is doing so.

I often feel blue. Mid-week blues hit you harder after you've enjoyed a long weekend road-tripping. It is like finding light at the end of a tunnel, but when you get to it, it is nothing but a light bulb, a dead end. The worst thing is not the false hope, the worst thing is that the light bulb is incandescent not LED, and now even Greta is disgusted by you.

But guess what, my life is going to be a road trip from now on.

I often wonder what if people could pursue different courses at different times in their lives. How hilarious would it be if a doctor behaves like a lawyer, or a dentist finally like a doctor?

I should have asked these questions prior to making one of the most expensive decisions of my life. If only Quora was live in those days.

I wonder if these unfortunate series of events in my life could be undone and if I could have the option to choose my career again, would anything be different? I was surrounded by such thoughts quite a lot, more so after a stretched vacation or a bad day at office!

The carefree life of kids makes me jealous. They don't live in constant fear of rejection and judgement. They don't have to think of the consequences and ramifications of their acts.

They just let it be. There is no security. The colourful picture we call life is fucked and is completely staged against you, and in the end all we need for a good night's sleep is our mother's warm hug.

We always settle for less!

Like how we serve our guests on the best plates but feed ourselves off the worst. You would settle for a career choice that might not be yours but someone else's. If you come from a middle-class family, it will most certainly be your family's.

But at Ricky's Beach Shack, we question. We question why we settle so soon and why we settle for less.

Don't seek fulfilling work in jobs that help you buy big cars. If the car you drove got you respect, then Mercedes drivers should apparently be ruling nations. Every Journalism major should be on prime time, spreading hate and venom in the form of debate. The nation wants you to suck it. Bitch.

So if I leave my house believing that everyone should support me and that it is everyone's support that will take me to the top or make me want to do things, then I am highly mistaken as it will not happen for sure. Rather, the most unexpected people, whom you might not trust in the first go and believe that they might not want to become a part of your journey, will eventually become an indispensable part of your career.

This one's for you Ricky, I point to him. *Thank you for everything.* Then, I look at Alara. She is one of the reasons I'm standing here, oozing out confidence. I adjust my eyes to notice that my family is making way through the crowd! My dad waves at me. Gosh! Uncle Ricky can be so unpredictable at times. But he is the best.

I have been through bad times. But am I the only one? No. Each one of us faces some sort of issues in our lives, and I am just one of you in the crowd. No different.

Except, I believe that I survived. I have handled the issue better than most people. I believe I handled it really well. Have I been on medication before? Well yes, I have gone through some sleeping issues in the past. To fix that issue I started using an app, and it turned out that I got addicted to that app, and ironically I started to use it all night. It was like curing cocaine addiction with heroin, but it was never the kind that my friends would be wary of! Over the last couple of months though, I have fallen sick.

215

You might now picture me sitting at a clinic and talking about my issues. Well, it is not so!

When heartbreak tore me apart, Ricky suggested that I use my vulnerability as a strength and explore my art. Sometimes, choosing a career all over again can be more empowering than failing to choose one in the first place, as now you know exactly why you are walking down this path and how important this path is.

And now, the most practical people like my papa would also cry and feel good about me when they see my capacity to make people laugh and cry.

I point to each one at Ricky's, my new home. There is no greater joy than falling back on those who will always be there for you. Maybe that's the reason why your heart belongs to your loved ones, your home, even if you are miles apart.

I love you all. You make me complete. The passion, the fear, the struggles, the setbacks; it is yet a dream—to become a stand-up comedian! This is me.

That's my time folks! Happy New Year!

As I walk down the stage, the salty breeze of the sea resonates with claps. Alara kisses me on the cheek.

'You're a rock star!' she says.

'You have always been one,' I reply as she makes her way to the stage. My dad walks up to me and hugs me.

'I am proud of you, *beta*!' he says and apologizes through his expressions.

'I love you, dad!'

'Is she your girlfriend?' he asks teasingly, like a typical middle-class Indian man in his sixties.

'Kind of!' I say and dodge the question. We aren't so comfortable speaking of our relationship in front of our families yet, you see.

Alara walks up the stage with our emotional Ricky and says:

It's beneath the blue sky and by the deep ocean where I looked for you. It's in the period after sunset and before sunrise when I looked for you. It's at my home and on islands far off where I looked for you. I could never find you elsewhere until I discovered you within. Oh! Happiness, it's been a long journey seeking you. I wish you were as simple to stumble upon as the clouds of sorrow in my heavy heart. Now that you're here, I will never let you go. You were as good as taking a decision and now I shall choose to be happy.

This one is dedicated to my mother.

She loves the mountain.
He loves the sea.
They decide to travel
twice together every year.

In the middle of nowhere,
sky above and ocean beneath,
they shout out loud
life is sea.

It is with life
as it is with waves,
the rise and fall
are endless.

The old pal says
that water enlightens
in every form.
Raindrop, tear,
hazy or clear.

Good food is a cure
for the ailing heart.
Why don't you try
my pizzas for a start?

They laugh, they cry
they sing in joy
Ricky's is where
life finds a way

As the spotlight moves from her and the faces in the audience become clear, she notices Parvathi cheering for her in the crowd. She makes her way to her and hugs her. I join them happily.

'I am sorry, Parvathi. I misunderstood you the other day. I'm really thankful to you for making me stay here in Goa and live like my mother. If I had known the truth the very first day when I met you, I would have left for Czech right away.'

'Alara, friends are meant to do that. I am fortunate that I crossed paths with you and learned so much from you. You're like family for us here in Goa.'

'Thank you for everything.'

'Mom called up your dad and told him everything. He knows that you won't speak to him for some time. He has read your message. He wants you to stay in Goa and release the much-awaited album. He also said that he feels sorry and wants to see you as soon as you feel better.'

'Yes, I will get back when I feel better. For now, let's order pizzas and drinks. It is the New Year!' she shouts out aloud.

I witness their conversation without uttering a word. I am so happy to see that Alara has finally decided to forgive, even if she doesn't forget everything that has happened. I can't wait for the day when the world would get to know the true story of Elisha, and the love of my life Alara will release her debut album. Uncle Ricky's going to be as crazy as he is! But I'm happy to have a mentor like him. Goa is all smiles tonight.

That's why they say, New Year's is the best time to be in Goa.

Alara walks up to me and says, 'The world is our home. It is delusional to call your apartment home. Even worse to stick to the same place all through your life. If you've found love or happiness somewhere, you've found a home.'

'I'm happy you've found a home. I have found one in you, too. It feels like I have heard these lines before.'

'My favourite blogger Ramy wrote this sometime back on his blog *on the open road*!'

'Oh, yes!'

It's never too late to start with the things that have been pending on your To-Do list for too long. All you have to do is start. It's a beautiful New Year's Eve, start today, now! You'll certainly feel victorious at the end of the year. Sometimes it's about achieving small goals to be happy and letting them sum up to bigger ones.

Everything falls into place if only you give your everything to it. The best way to overcome all your fears is to realize them.

EPILOGUE

(Six months later)

21 June 2020

Every Sunday, I take a walk to the orphanage from Ricky's after my morning run. I don't really buy flowers on the way. I mostly do that for Sheen on the weekdays. Friends become demanding when they turn into wives! I handpick the flowers from the park at the orphanage itself.

Today is special indeed. It is Elisabeth's 41st birthday. As I reach the park and take my seat near the gravestone, I am reminded that we had spent her 14th birthday in the park itself. Time flies.

While I can never forgive myself for not coming back when she needed me, I make this effort to tell myself that my intentions were never wrong. Love made me do things I never knew I was capable of. Beautiful mostly. Ugly too.

Alara visits here often but we've never crossed paths. We choose to be here on our own. After all, we all have our own things to talk about in peace hoping that Elisha, wherever she is, understands a bit of how much we love her.

'Your wish is my command,' I say as I offer the handpicked flowers. 'Although I would have been happier if we recorded this album together, your daughter, she is just as crazy as you were. Aarav handles her well. I'll get them married. I won't let Aarav make the same mistake as I did. I'm liking my married life. Sheen understands most of what I don't say. She isn't mean like you. I am leaving early today, I have to be at the launch in the evening. I have to catch the flight to Mumbai. Bye. See you next week.'

As I stand at Elisha's grave, I say goodbye to her. This bond—magical, fulfilling, and deep—will last in my memories forever. I have a piece of her wherever I go and she will have a piece of me until the end of time.

Goodbyes are hard. Aren't they?

If you still haven't expressed your love to someone, don't wait for too long! Walk up to them today. You don't wish to end up like me. Do you?

As Sheen and I reach the launch venue, we find Alara already present. While they're dressed up formally, I am in my Goan shirt and shorts. Media has mostly gathered by now so has a huge crowd, Alara's fans mostly. Since we announced the launch of our album on *YouTube* along with the real story of Elisha, media has been chasing us like crazy. Alara is quite a sensation in the music industry now.

Alara and I make way towards the stage. Shantanu, our producer from Mumbai, also makes his way to it.

A volunteer walks up to us and adjusts our mics. There's a table in front of us. Alara holds my hand beneath the table and we look at each other. We're happy that we can do this for Elisha. Wherever she is, she would be delighted to see us. The media starts to question us. By the way, I am a lot more confident now. 'Sunrise to Sunset' aired last month and Ricky's has become the most popular place in Goa.

'Why did you give the title 'You Only Live Once?' to the album? '

Alara smiles at me, indicating that she would take this up. I agree with a nod.

'It is told to us, time and again, that we only live once. It means, live life to the fullest, cease the day! We agree to that. But once we put a question mark to it, we want to ask people, do we really live only once? We live in the hearts of people years after we die. While our physical bodies may live only once, a part of us stays alive in people's memories forever. We're not the same for each one of them as we leave a different impact on their lives. While our life is important, how we choose to live it is equally important. We want people to reflect on what impact they would want to leave on the lives of other people when they're gone. The songs are in sync with our thoughts.'

'Your songs touch upon themes like depression. Why did you choose it?'

'To be able to see the colours around us, sometimes it's essential to eliminate the darkness within. The world isn't actually how it is, the world is how we see it. If we're optimistic and positive in general, the world reflects our thoughts like a mirror. If we're negative in general, it's the same! Understanding this and working on it can help us conquer the most negative of emotions. If my mother could have done it, she would have been sitting in my place today, launching her album on her birthday.'

One of the media persons interrupts, 'Are you dating the famous stand-up comedian Aarav?'

'Yes. We're dating. He would have been here, but he is in Singapore for his first ever standalone stand-up act out of India. He will join us in Goa tomorrow.'

'Is it true that you've shifted to Goa? Do you plan to go back to Czech?'

'I feel I belong here. I never went back to Czech and have no plans to do so in the near future. I will be shuttling between Mumbai and Goa. Ricky and Sheen are my new family. I want to stay as close to my mother as possible.

Elisha's story has brought us together and helped us move in a new direction.'

I adjust my mic as I say jokingly, 'All the questions for the pretty lady. You guys have nothing to ask me? I have played the drums.' The hall echoes with laughter.

'Is it true that you were in love with Elisha?'

'Yes. Can you ask me questions that make sense? Why are you focusing on our personal lives only?' I shout back.

Alara holds my hand firmly and gestures at me to tone down.

'With your first album being such a huge hit even prior to its release, what does the future hold for you?'

I reply, 'This is just the beginning. We will be working on many more original compositions together.'

'Alara, you recently met RR Maan, a stalwart of the music industry. How was your experience?'

'It was so engrossing to listen to his songs and stories around recording and performing. When I asked him what has been his greatest learning from a singing career spanning across decades, all he summed up for me was, listen to everyone but follow your heart. He told me that while everyone suggested that he should release a sad song as his debut single, he went against the common idea and released it as an upbeat music number instead. We all know that it rose to the top of the charts, and the rest is history.'

After an hour of playing question and answer with them, and signing for innumerous fans, Alara and I head to the airport.

On the flight, while we sit quietly next to each other, and without looking at me, Alara starts to talk.

'Ricky, I am so at peace today. Six months ago, for a moment I thought I had lost my purpose, my dream, my mother. But now I realize that her life is far bigger than what she lived. Her songs bring her alive in me, in us.'

Author's Note

Feeling Inspired?

Please leave a review on Amazon, Flipkart and Goodreads. It will help me reach out to more readers who can be inspired to touch people's lives with their ideas!

If you'd like, also share your thoughts on social media using #stutichangle, #SCFamily

Acknowledgements

First and foremost, to my readers who make me live my dream. All the love you've showered upon me, gave me the courage to sail through this bumpy entrepreneurial journey.

A special one for my younger brother, Swapnil Changle, for helping me develop the snippets of stand-up comedy. I felt that the journey of a comedian would be incomplete without some of his performances. While I could write the songs on my own, this one would have been incomplete without you. You've spared time from your late night shifts and it really means a lot to me.

Kushal Nahata, the love of my life, whom I met in Goa exactly where this story is set. We tied the knot recently. I can't thank him enough for believing in me and my love for storytelling. He is a successful entrepreneur and I really look up to him as a guide and a mentor.

Mom and Dad, for bringing me into this world and not abandoning me despite my unconventional career choice. My dreams would not have seen the light of day without your love.

My in-laws, my new family, who support me as their very own daughter. I am fortunate to have precisely four parents take care of me now.

My Naniji, the only living grandparent, for loving me unconditionally and teaching me to live life to the fullest.

Lucky, my dog who I lost in the summer of 2014, for teaching me the meaning of love. After you passed away, I came to know that there are some voids that can never be filled. You are always in my thoughts and prayers. I wish you were here to see me as a successful author.

Vivek Ranjan, my selfless and hustler manager, who takes care of all the other things so I can focus more on my creative work. This book wouldn't have been complete without you.

Awatar Kishan and Pushkar Singh, who give an added dimension to my stories through enthralling book covers. I am so in love with your work that I want to say, 'Let's start working on the third book's cover right away.'

Amit Singhal, for giving me the opportunity to host my first ever TV show. I have learnt so much in this new journey while interacting with one of the best entrepreneurs in the country. Mentors like you power the start-up community.

Anshu Mor, for being there at my first book launch and making it a huge success. For such humility even after becoming a star stand-up comedian. I look up to you.

My friends, Shefali Gupta, Shivani Chauhan, Mohi Sharma, Vanshika Sha, Harry Sandhu, Shristi Dubey, Gaurav Srivastava, who stick with me through thick and thin. These are a few names to begin with, honestly, there's a long list here. I am thankful to the Universe for having met such amazing people.

My fans from the social media community who encourage me to do more. #SCFamily, #stutichangle is growing every day, pushing me to work harder.

Dev and Chandni, co-founders of Voice of Slum, for giving me a reason and an opportunity to give back to the society. Souls like you help build a better tomorrow.

To my passion and never-ending love for travelling that took me to Goa. I fell in love with the beauty of Canacona, kept going back every year, eight times and counting. I could picturize Goa so well in this story because of that.

To the stars and nature for their clarion call to look till infinity and beyond, to inspiring scientists, poets, writers, artists—practically, each one of us alike.

Acknowledgements

To the board in Starbucks, where I completed this book as well, that read, 'Extraordinary things come from tiny beans.'

Love, Stuti